DARK BLOWS THE WIND

When Anne Taverne finds a wounded Cavalier in the orchard, she conceals him in the house. Later that evening the house is searched by a stern-faced Roundhead colonel who is so bewitched by Anne that he fails to discover his hidden enemy. As the Civil War progresses Anne becomes increasingly involved with these two men, but she is totally unprepared for the bewildering world of conflicting loyalties and emotional battles in which she finds herself enmeshed.

LYNN GRANVILLE

◆

DARK BLOWS THE WIND

Complete and Unabridged

LINFORD
Leicester

2016

First published in Great Britain in 1984

First Linford Edition
published 1998

British Library CIP Data

Granville, Lynn
    Dark blows the wind.—Large print ed.—
    Linford romance library
    1. Love stories
    2. Large type books
    I. Title
    823.9'14 [F]

    ISBN 0–7089–5300–X

Published by
F. A. Thorpe (Publishing) Ltd.
Anstey, Leicestershire

Set by Words & Graphics Ltd.
Anstey, Leicestershire
Printed and bound in Great Britain by
T. J. International Ltd., Padstow, Cornwall

This book is printed on acid-free paper

1

OUTSIDE I could hear the wind's howl and the relentless rain driving against the windows. I shivered, hating the sound, though safe inside my home I had no fear of the storm itself. A Tudor manor house, its red bricks and timber frame mellowed by time, Withington had withstood many storms. Here in this house I had always been protected, sheltered, loved . . .

Casting my eyes towards the bed where the grandmother I loved lay dying, I felt a premonition that my secure world was about to be torn apart, that the years of my childhood were somehow behind me. For hours now I had sat beside Sarah Taverne's bed watching the play of shadows on the wall as the candle flickered and burned low, straining to catch the faint sound of her breathing.

There was a movement from the bed and I leaned forward as Sarah turned her face towards me, whispering my name, 'Anne, my dear child . . . ' Her lips moved in what I knew was a blessing, then she was gone from this life and from me. She went without a struggle to the arms of her Maker, secure in the knowledge of His love, content to trust in Him in death as she had in life — and her going left an aching emptiness inside me.

Bending to close her staring eyes, I kissed her cheek for the last time and whispered a prayer. Then, hearing a stifled moan, I looked across the bed at the man sitting there, seeing the lines of pain and grief in his face.

'You must not grieve, Grandfather,' I said, knowing as I spoke I wasted my breath. 'She would not want it so. It was a blessed relief for her.'

Sir John's head moved in denial of my statement. He covered his face with blue-veined hands which shook

2

with the force of his emotion, and I knew he was fighting a battle within himself. Even as he acknowledged the truth of my words, his heart cried out at the pain of his loss. I understood what was passing through his mind, though he made no sound. Forty years of loving were not enough: he wanted one more year, a day — even an hour. I understood because in my heart I, too, was protesting at this cruel loss.

Moving to his side my hand hovered above his bowed shoulders and then fell. Much as I longed to comfort him, I knew my sympathy would be more than he could bear just now. He needed to be alone with his beloved wife so that he could give way to his grief without shame.

'I will go down to Prudence,' I said, receiving no answer and expecting none.

As I closed the door behind me I heard his first, painful sob. He had held back his grief for so long, fearing to hurt Sarah with his tears. Now she was gone he could shed them at last.

My throat felt tight and tears stung my eyes as I realised that it was all over. Those terrible weeks of watching my dearest friend suffer bravely through her pain were finished. I could weep now if I chose and she would not feel my pain. Yet there was Prudence to consider. Downstairs my sister sat alone in the parlour and I knew I must be strong for her. Prudence had always been delicate, finding sickness and death almost more than her gentle nature could bear. She would need to be comforted.

Brushing away my tears, I assumed the mantle of calm assurance I habitually wore when I wanted to calm Prudence's fears. Two years ago our mother had died giving birth to a still-born son. Worn out by constant miscarriages and ill health, her body had finally given up the unequal struggle. Prudence had been wild with grief then, making herself so frail with weeping that we feared for her life. That must not happen this time. I would not let it happen. I loved my sister too dearly to lose her too.

Without Sarah life at Withington would be hard enough to bear in these times of civil war when half the countryside were our enemies. Although I still rode into the village to see my friend Mercy Harris, the widow of a country gentleman fallen on hard times, I was aware of the hostility in some of the cottagers' eyes. I could not afford to lose my sister just yet; though I knew she would marry one day for she was far prettier than I.

My face was thin, the skin stretched taughtly over high checkbones; though my colour was good. I had thick, dark hair and a mouth I considered too wide; but my eyes were my one attractive feature. They were deep blue and glowing with life, sometimes sparkling with passion when I was roused to joy or anger.

I knew as I walked down the wide staircase that some of my concern for

Prudence was selfishness. I had seen enough sickness and pain these past weeks to last me a lifetime — but was not love always a little selfish? Few of us are able to give that truly unselfish love which requires no return — though I had been privileged to know one such person.

Somehow Sarah had always known whenever there was sickness or need in the village, and she had found a way of helping; doing so in such a manner that the cottagers felt no shame in accepting her bounty. It had been the same with her family. With Sarah it was possible to confide one's innermost fears without feeling naked or stripped of pride. Oh, how I would miss her!

Pausing for a moment, I bent my head to inhale the sweet fragrance from a vase of roses I had picked this morning while the dew was on them. It was my habit to fill every available niche with flowers from my garden whenever I could. Even in the winter I searched the woods for branches bearing bright berries, for of all things I loved best the treasures God had given us.

Next to my garden I loved Withington. Built when Good Queen Bess was still at the beginning of her glorious reign, it was not one of those empty, echoing mansions with endless passages where the wind finds every crack in the wainscot. It was a family home rather than tribute to the first Taverne's pride, the rooms centred around a large hall. My grandfather had panelled the walls with solid English oak when he was first wed, and his library boasted a carpet of many colours from far-off Persia. At the tiny leaded windows were soft drapes to keep out the winter chill. It was a place of warmth, memories and laughter — but now the laughter — had gone.

As I reached the parlour door, pausing for a moment to gather my courage, shadows from the firelight flickered on panelled oak, twisting

7

the geometrical patterns into grotesque shapes the carpenter had never intended — or perhaps it was only the demons of self-doubt dancing in my mind.

Prudence was sitting on a joint stool before the fire, staring into the flames, tension in every line of her body. At the sound of my footsteps she looked round, her eyes widening in fear.

She rose slowly to her feet, her face pale. 'I was cold so I asked Greta to light the fire,' she said, her voice trailing away to a thin whisper. 'Is — is Sarah . . . ?

There was no way to ease her pain. I could only hold out my arms to her as I said, 'Yes.'

She took a step towards me, her face crumpling. 'Oh no. No . . . '

Tears began to well up in her lovely eyes, spilling over the fair lashes to tumble down her cheeks. She pressed her hand against her mouth as if trying to hold back the scream building inside her, and I saw terror in her face.

At that moment my thoughts were

only for Prudence; I felt her pain and horror as if it were my own. She was only a child, little more than sixteen. It was too much for her.

Crossing the floor quickly, I drew her into my arms. Giving her a little shake, I held her tightly as I felt the shudders run through her slight body. Stroking her light brown hair, I did my best to comfort her, loving her more in our shared loss than perhaps ever before.

'Hush, dearest, do not hurt yourself so. It is for the best. You know I'm right.'

Prudence leant against me weakly, weeping. 'I loved her so much, Anne. What shall I do?'

I closed my eyes, despair washing over me. How could I answer her when I felt so lost myself? Fears for the future haunted my mind — not only for us but for Grandfather and Withington itself. England was in the middle of a bloody war which had torn men from the heart of their families. Our father had ridden off the day after his wife's funeral, promising to return once the King was safely restored to his throne. Since then we had had but two letters from him, the last some six months ago. For all we knew Saul Taverne might be lying in an unmarked grave like so many others.

But I knew I must not let Prudence guess how uncertain I was. Soon the war might be over and then our father would come home. Our lives could never be the same again now that mother and Sarah were gone, but I was fast learning that life goes on despite grief. I could only pray it would not be too long before father returned, for Sir John had received a grievous blow and Sarah's illness had aged him terribly. He was not the man who had sent his son to war with a smile and brave words.

I knew that the King was losing the war, though Grandfather would not have it so. But I had heard the gossip in the village and Mercy had told me things did not go well for

His Majesty. As the war between King and Parliament grew ever more bitter houses had been burnt to the ground and families forced to flee for their lives. In the village some of the women were wearing black, weeping for sons and husbands who would never return. I dare not think what might happen to Withington if Saul did not come back.

Prudence had stopped crying. I released her, depressed by the headache I had been fighting all day. I had been at Sarah's bedside for hours and now it was time for me to seek my own release. I needed some fresh air in my lungs.

'I think I shall go for a walk.'

Prudence looked startled. 'It's a dreadful night, Anne — you will be blown off your feet.'

Shaking my head, I smiled at her. 'I don't mind the wind — and the rain must have stopped for I can no longer hear it beating against the windows. I shall go only as far as the orchard. I shall not be long.' I walked to the door and then looked back at her, hesitating but knowing what must be said. 'Grandfather needs to be alone with Sarah for a time — but there are things needful to be done. I shall not allow the maids to care for her, though Bessie can help me.'

I saw a flicker of pain pass across my sister's face and I was sorry for her. Sarah's death was hard enough for me to bear, how much worse then was it for Prudence.

'I shall not go up to — to pay my respects until you say I may, Anne.'

I smiled gently. 'We shall go together, my love.'

Prudence sighed. Picking up a heavy, religious tome Sir John had left lying open on the table, she flicked nervously through the pages.

'Take your cloak if you go out — Bessie says the wind is cold tonight.' She shivered. 'No one would think it was June!'

I saw the effort she was making to contain her grief and I wondered if I ought to stay with her a little longer; but my head was throbbing now and I longed to be alone for a while.

'I shall not be long,' I promised, going out into the hall before Prudence's wan smile should persuade me to stay.

The hall was a wide, square chamber at the heart of the house, flanked on one side by Sir John's library and the dining-room, and by the parlour and the kitchens on the other. When I was a tiny child Withington had often been full of guests, and it was in the hall they had gathered of an evening to talk and laugh or listen to music. My mother sometimes sang to her friends for her voice had been sweet and clear like a yaffingale; but those happy days belonged to the past. It was many years since my parents had held a party at Withington, and the only guests who came to dine these days were old friends of Sir John's. Yet I had never felt lonely whilst Sarah was alive.

Taking a cloak from the mule chest

set in a recess beneath the stairs, I put it on, drawing the fur-trimmed hood over my head. As I went out of a side door into the courtyard, the fury of the wind caught me off-guard, lifting my cloak and tugging it away from my body. For a moment I stood still, debating if I should return to the parlour. It was a wild night for walking and the howl of the wind had an evil sound. Shivering, I pulled my cloak closer. Perhaps I would merely take a turn about the courtyard to relieve the worst of my headache, yet I needed to be away from the house for a while. A brisk walk was what I needed and the wind would blow away the smell of sickness and death.

I suppose what I really needed was a good cry, but I had held my feelings in check for so long I could not release them now. Watching Sarah gradually waste away had been hard. Outwardly I had remained calm and cheerful, but I think Sarah had seen the pain I tried to hide. It was she who had been brave to the last, making us laugh through the darkest days.

Tucking my head down against the wind, I navigated the tiny, crooked path between the herb garden and the lavender bushes, catching their rain-fresh scent as I passed. It was here I spent some or my happiest hours planting flowers. Love-in-a-mist, honesty and those strange, waxy flowers called tulips were some of my latest acquisitions. But perhaps one of my greatest treasures was a book entitled *Paradise* which Sarah had given me for my twentieth birthday, sending for a copy to London specially. It praised and described various flowers, and was very popular just now. Despite the war Englishwomen continued to enjoy their gardens be they humble or grand. Like most other country women I knew the names of many herbs, and those which would be helpful to me in my stillroom, but I was always looking for fresh recipes. I had great belief in the healing properties of my

15

herbs — though I had found nothing which could help Sarah.

Sarah had loved flowers too. I could see her now in my mind sitting by the parlour window wrapped in a warm shawl, watching as I worked and smiling as I paused now and then to wave at her.

The scent of the flowers brought a sharp reminder and I gasped as I felt the pain twist inside me. I was going to miss Sarah so much! My hand trembled on the iron latch of the gate leading to the orchard and I felt the rain sting my eyes — or was it tears? I scrubbed at my face impatient of what I considered weakness. I had to be strong for my sister's sake.

For a moment I stood unmoving, feeling the wind lash at my body. The trees were waving to and fro in a wild frenzy as the storm gathered renewed fury. I shivered as a cold chill trickled along my spine. It was then I heard the sound. At first I thought it merely the wind or a trick of my mind;

then it came again more clearly and I knew it was a human being in pain. The cry had come from somewhere close by, probably the other side of the garden wall. Acting on impulse, I went through the gate into the orchard, turning towards the sound.

As if to help me the moon chose that moment to slip from behind the clouds and I saw the dark shape of a man lying on the ground a few feet away. I moved towards him hesitantly at first, uncertain of what to do. Who was he and how came he to be in our orchards? He lay still as I bent over him, groaning. I knelt down beside him on the wet earth, putting out my hand to touch him. He was lying on his stomach, his face hidden from me, but I could see the fair hair straggling in his neck. He did not move as I touched him, so I took hold of his shoulder, rolling him carefully on to his back. His eyes flickered open, his lips moving as he tried to speak.

'Do not be alarmed,' I said, noticing

the dark stain on his coat and recognising it for what it was. He had been badly wounded and he had lost a great deal of blood. I thought he looked close to death and I felt a sickness in my throat. Surely one death tonight was enough! I stood up, wanting to run — the servants could deal with this. 'I'm going to fetch help for you, sir. Someone will come . . .'

As I tried to rise he took hold of my wrist, his fingers closing round it weakly. I smiled at him, knowing he was afraid I would desert him.

'I will send help; do not doubt me.'

But he did doubt me. A spasm of fear passed across his face and somehow he forced the words out: 'No . . . you help me.'

'I'm not strong enough to lift you,' I protested, but already he had rolled on to his side and was trying to rise, his pale face a ghastly mask of pain. 'You should not . . .'

I watched helplessly as he struggled painfully to his knees, slumped to the ground with a groan and rose again. But now my first panic had evaporated and somehow his courage had touched a chord within me. I no longer wanted to run from him and my only fear was that he might harm himself by his foolishness. As he swayed again I took hold of his shoulder steadying him. He grabbed my arm, using it to drag himself to his feet. I felt the weight of his body pulling on me and cried out as he almost toppled me. Then I recovered my balance, stooping so that his arm slid across my back as I half lifted him to a standing position. In that moment I knew he was too heavy for me: I would never get him to the house alone.

'I cannot,' I said, terrified he would fall and carry me with him. I could not help him if I was pinioned beneath his body. 'Let me fetch help I beg you.'

But from somewhere deep inside himself he had found new strength. He shook his head, looking down at me with a grimace which might have been a grin. I saw then that his face was young and well formed. I should probably have thought him handsome if I had not been angry with him for forcing me to struggle beneath his weight instead of fetching help.

'I can walk,' he muttered between clenched teeth.

And he did walk if only to spite me, leaning heavily on my shoulders as I staggered towards the house. Twice he stumbled nearly taking me down with him, but each time he recovered his balance, forcing himself to stay upright by will-power alone.

Almost against my will I was moved by his courage. I believed him a Royalist by his look and the feel of his doublet, but I would have taken him in now if he had been a Roundhead. I suppose I understood the causes of the war as well as most, having read the newsletters which came down from London and were passed from house to house; but the King's folly in abusing Parliament's rights by raising unjust taxes, and

Laud's egotistical leanings towards the Roman church meant little to me. I had heard my grandfather discussing politics with his friends and I knew he was a confirmed Royalist, therefore, I was a Royalist, too; but for myself the war meant only that my father was away fighting and might lose his life, and that people I had known all my life turned their heads when they saw me.

'It isn't far now,' I said, as much to encourage myself as the man I was helping. 'But I do not know how we shall get you upstairs . . .'

He made no reply and I guessed it was taking all his strength just to stay upright. Reaching the house, I shifted his weight against the wall as I struggled with the latch, taking it back again as we went inside.

It was with a sense of relief that I saw Prudence had heard the door and come out into the hall. She stared at me, her mouth dropping open as she saw me swaying beneath my burden and I shouted at her.

'Help me, Prue — I think he's going to fall!'

'He's bleeding . . . ' She said, her face white. 'Anne — who is he?'

My patience snapped. 'Never mind that, just help me!'

Prudence made no move towards me and I was about to yell at her again when Bessie Goodram appeared out of the shadows at the far end of the hall.

'I'll help you, Mistress Anne,' she said, coming quickly to relieve me. 'He's too heavy for Mistress Prudence. I'm strong, let me have him. I've put me Pa to bed many's the night when the drink's taken him. I can manage this scrap of a lad easy enough.'

I smiled wryly. The wounded man was no lad, but Bessie was a stout woman and her strength was undoubted. She worked harder than most men and rumour had it she was so strong no man in the village had dared to offer for her as a young girl. But I knew the real reason she had never wed was her devotion to the Taverne family, in particular Prudence and myself. She had helped bring us into this world and thought of us as her own family.

I was grateful for her timely arrival, thanking her as I passed the bulk of the stranger's weight to her. My shoulders had begun to ache and I knew I could never have got him upstairs alone.

'Where shall we put him?' Bessie asked as we reached the landing. 'None of the spare beds have been slept in these many months — they'll need airing unless he's to die of pneumonia.'

'He can have my bed for tonight — I can sleep with Prudence. In the morning we'll transfer him to the secret room — if he's still alive. I think that might be wiser.'

Bessie nodded, a grim look on her plump face. 'I thought as much — what will you be at next, Mistress Anne? Is it not bad enough Sir John is nigh the only Royalist in the district without you harbouring strangers?'

'Only one stranger, Bessie,' I replied,

smiling slightly. 'Would you have had me leave him to die?'

'Well, don't blame me if he brings the Roundheads down on us,' she grumbled.

I frowned. 'Do you think the servants will talk of this in the village?'

Bessie's eyes sparkled with the light of battle. 'There's none in this house as would betray you — lest they deal with me first!'

'He's badly wounded and like to die of it — what harm can he do anyone?' I asked, but I was remembering the fear on his face when I tried to fetch help. What had he to be afraid of?

I pulled back the covers and we laid him in my bed. His face was so pale I feared he was already dead; but pressing my ears to his heart I heard a faint beating. He was alive but only just. If I had not found him when I did he would have been dead by morning. I shivered as I recalled how close I had come to returning to the parlour instead of taking my walk.

It was a matter of urgency his wound be dressed as he was still loosing blood. Once he was settled in the bed, Bessie hurried away to fetch clean linen and a pan of hot water, while I stared at him wondering who he was and how he had come to be at my gate. Perhaps he'd been involved in a battle. Had there been fighting nearby today?

Bessie returned with the linen and we began to cut away his clothes. He seemed to have lost consciousness and we were thankful he was unaware of our actions, for we must have caused him pain moving him as we did.

'You had best let me finish,' Bessie said when we had stripped away his buff coat and velvet doublet. 'It is not fitting that you should tend a naked man — 'tis bad enough he's in your bed.'

I raised my brows at her. 'What matter as long as I am not in it with him,' I asked, knowing I was shocking her. 'Oh, don't fuss so, Bessie, I've washed Sally Lucas's boys many times.

I shan't faint at the sight of a male body I promise you.'

'The Lucas boys are children,' Bessie replied, her mouth set in a stubborn line. 'Turn your back if you won't leave. I'll tell you when he's decent.'

I knew Bessie was perfectly capable of arguing for hours so rather than waste time I did as I was told, bending to pick up the stranger's discarded shirt and coat. As I did so a small roll of parchment fell out on to the floor. I picked it up, wiping away the smears of blood and laying it on the table beside the bed. For a moment I wondered whether it was important, then I forgot it as Bessie spoke.

'All right, you can look now.'

I turned to see the bedcovers had been arranged discreetly over the lower half of the man's body. I might have been amused by Bessie's care for my modesty if I had not seen the terrible wound in the stranger's side. It was deep and jagged, and looked as though it might have been inflicted by the point of a pikestaff.

Shuddering, I poured water into a bowl, holding it for Bessie as she began to sponge away the blood. It was difficult because fresh blood oozed from the gash in his side all the time and the water in my bowl soon turned crimson. Pushing the torn flesh together as best she could, she pressed a wad of linen hard against his wound, bidding me to hold it steady whilst she wound the bandages around his chest.

The pressure seemed to help a little for the white bandages did not immediately turn crimson. Bessie sighed as she finished her work, collecting the bloody cloths in her bowl. 'There's no more I can do for him — 'tis in the hands of God now.'

I knew she was right. 'If he lives through the night I'll send word to Doctor Babbage. I think we can trust him. He may not be as determined a Royalist as Sir John but he has been my grandfather's friend for as long as

I can remember.'

Bessie shrugged. 'Aye, ask him to call for all the good it will do. Now, I'd best get rid of these cloths before anyone sees them.' She looked at me and her face softened. 'Will you be wanting help with your grandmother, child?'

For a moment I could only stare at her. In the struggle to bring the injured man to safety I had forgotten what had happened here this evening. Now the memory swept through me, bringing fresh pain. I turned my head aside, hiding the sudden tears.

'Yes — in a little while,' I mumbled, trying to hold back my tears.

'Weep, child, there's no shame in it,' Bessie said kindly. 'I'll be back soon.'

Bessie went out and I brushed away my tears. I wasn't going to cry; there was still much to be done before I could creep into bed beside Prudence.

I glanced down at the stranger lying in my bed. He seemed to be breathing easily now and he had not stirred since

Bessie tucked the covers around him. We had done all we could for him tonight, there was no point in my staying longer. Yet I was reluctant to leave. He looked so helpless, so young . . .

Sighing, I was about to depart when I remembered the piece of parchment I had found. Picking it up I looked at it thoughtfully before slipping it into the bodice of my gown. I would read it if the stranger died.

* * *

We did not move our uninvited guest into the secret room the next morning, for when I went to look at him on rising I discovered he was burning up with a fever. His skin was damp and hot when I touched him and he was tossing restlessly. I was frightened he would open the wound in his side again and I went in search of Bessie to confide my fears to her. She was in the still-room busily preparing the first of the primrose wine when I found her. Her brows went up and she shook her head as I told her why I had come.

''Tis not good, Mistress Anne . . . ' she broke off as the scullery maid came in.

Bessie scowled at her. 'Yes — what do you want, girl?'

Greta dropped a hasty curtsey to me. 'Begging your pardon, Mistress Anne, but Mr Hoddle sent me to find you. The doctor be come to see Sir John and he do be shut up in his library and vows he will see no one. Mr Hoddle do say as he have done his best to reason with Sir John — but the master be set in his mind.'

I nodded. Hoddle was Sir John's personal body servant and the relation-ship stretched over many years, the servant almost as obstinate as his master. If Hoddle could not budge Sir John I knew there was little use in my trying. He would come when he was ready and not before.

'Thank you, Greta.' I smiled at the

girl. 'I will go to the doctor myself.'

Greta curtsied again, shot a scared glance at Bessie and scampered away.

I turned to Bessie. 'Fate must be on our side. I shall ask Doctor Babbage to look at our guest before he leaves.'

'Aye, if you will, though the man's a charlatan. The apothecary from the village would be of more use. I'll send a groom for one of his fever mixtures this morn' — there's no need to say who 'tis for. Who's to know Mistress Prudence isn't poorly again?'

I pulled a wry face at her. 'Do not tempt fate, Bessie. I had fain have Prudence in full health. I think it was a comfort to her that we shared a bed last night and it will do no harm if we continue to do so for a time. She cried herself to sleep in my arms poor sweeting.'

'And wore you out with her wailing I've no doubt,' muttered Bessie, but I did not stay to listen. I was used to her grumbling and took little notice of it.

When I reached the parlour I found

Doctor Babbage already comfortably seated, talking with Prudence. She looked at me and I saw relief in her eyes, relief that she would no longer have to entertain him alone.

Doctor Babbage was a stout man of medium height with a florid complexion and a temper to match. I knew Prudence found his company tedious, but I rather liked him, though I was fully aware of his weaknesses. He loved wine, good food, horses and the companionship of his friends. He was too lazy to be either a Royalist or a Parliamentarian, for to care passionately for a cause would require too much effort. He wasn't a religious man and perhaps that was one reason I liked him since it made him less critical than many of his fellows. In our village we had a Puritan minister and I found his visits hard to bear, knowing he came only to lecture me. When he first came to Withington it had not been thus, but since the war he had blossomed in the new regime, showing his true colours. In less troubled times my grandfather might have sent him packing but for now we found it safer to bear with him. Babbage fortunately, never bothered to probe beneath the surface, and providing I did not plage him too much on behalf of some poor villager we agreed very well.

His eyes were anxious as he heaved himself to his feet and came towards me, taking my hands. 'This is a bad business, Mistress Anne. Pon my soul, I don't know what to say to you.'

I glanced at Prudence wondering if she had mentioned the wounded man upstairs, but she shook her head and I knew he was speaking of Sarah's death and Sir John's refusal to leave his library.

'Grandfather is overcome with grief, sir. I'm sure he will apologise to you another day. I'm sorry you've had a wasted journey.'

Babbage shook his head. ''Tis no matter — I came to tell him the news but I never thought to find this . . . '

33

His chins quivered. 'Grief is all very well in its place but it doesn't do to shut oneself from the world. Won't do I tell you!'

'No indeed, sir.' I took his arm persuasively, knowing his pompous manner hid a real concern for his friend. 'We shall endeavour to prevent it happening again — but may a man not have a little space for his grief? They were married for more than forty years.'

'H'rmm. Yes, of course, my dear.' The doctor's feathers settled as he smiled at me. I knew he was fond of me in his way and I suspected he might have asked me to be his wife had he been less inclined to indolence. I was glad he had not done so for I should have refused him and then I might have lost a good friend.

I smiled up at him as he patted my hand. 'But now you're here, there is something you can do for me if you will.'

His brows creased anxiously and I

knew he was afraid I meant to bully him about the villagers' well-being again. His patients were all members of the gentry and he had no love for the cottagers. On the rare occasions one of them sent for him he was reluctant to enter their homes, which were often little more than hovels and sometimes stank of urine and animal manure. The poorer amongst them had a habit of taking their swine into their homes during the winter since they had no other shelter for the beasts. But even if the cottages were clean and strewn with fresh rushes, the villagers had no money to pay him nor did they listen to his advice. I could hardly blame him for his reluctance to visit, though I continued to ask for his help on their behalf just as Sarah had done.

But now I had other matters on my mind and I was not quite sure how to begin. There were many Parliamentary supporters in the district and if it became known we had harboured a Royalist it might mean trouble for us — and for Doctor Babbage if he became involved. Perhaps I had no right to ask for his assistance, but without it I was afraid the man in my bed would die.

'There is a wounded man upstairs,' I said, deciding frankness was best. 'I believe he is a Royalist soldier. We have done what we can for him, but he has a fever and I think his wound needs attention. Will you examine him for me?'

A little to my surprise Doctor Babbage agreed at once; perhaps he was relieved to be let off so lightly. He smiled at me kindly. 'Of course, my dear — friend of Sir John's is he?'

I hesitated, then inclined my head. It was a small lie and would ensure his silence. I knew he would not betray a friend of my grandfather's.

He followed me up the stairs to the door of my bed-chamber, but when I would have gone in with him he prevented me with a shake of his head. 'I shall examine him alone, Mistress

Anne — it will be necessary to uncover him you know.'

'I shall wait in the parlour,' I replied, hiding my vexation. The doctor was extremely nice in his ideas of propriety and I could not distress him by destroying his good opinion of me. 'You will let me know how he is before you leave?'

'Most certainly, my dear.'

Retracing my steps to the parlour, I wondered why it was that an unmarried girl of my status was expected to remain so ignorant of the basic facts of life until her marriage. It was impossible to have attended my mother during two miscarriages and still be ignorant of the nature of marriage, or to have lived all my life in the country and not understand the cycle of creation. And yet it was presumed to look on a man's naked body would sully my innocence. I found it ridiculous, but I was enough the creature of my age to know my thoughts would shock the most liberal-minded of my friends so I kept them to myself. Indeed, sometimes I was shocked by the wickedness of my own thoughts. Especially when I listened to Parson Croxley ranting on about the fires of hell as he looked down on his congregation. Somehow I did not want to believe in Croxley's god. I resented being told I was a sinner because I did not conform to what was expected of me in this our new and glorious land.

In the parlour I found Prudence diligently working on a kerchief she was embroidering for our father. I put my troublesome thoughts from my mind and went to sit beside her, admiring her fine stitchery.

'I am making this for father,' she said, showing me the initials S.T. in the corner. 'Do you think he will be pleased with me?'

'I am sure he will — he will be surprised how much you've grown and how pretty you are.'

Prudence smiled. I was glad to see her busy and calm, even if I sensed she was not as happy as she seemed. At least she was making an effort to come to terms with her grief, as we all must. We did not speak of Sarah and neither of us could bear to look at her chair or the silent spinning-wheel in its corner.

In a short while Babbage came down again, his face grim. I went to meet him, my heart thumping in my breast. I knew the news was not good, but I did not know why it should mean so much to me.

'He's in a bad way, Mistress Anne. I've patched him up as best I can but . . . ' He shook his head at me. 'I cannot hold out much hope for him.'

I thanked him, pouring him a glass of wine. He drank it slowly, taking his time while I fretted with impatience for him to be gone so that I could go upstairs. Then he began to tell me why he had come to visit Grandfather and I knew how my Cavalier had come to be so gravely wounded.

'They say there was a fearful battle

at Naseby two days ago — God knows how many were killed or injured. 'Twas a victory for Parliament and Cromwell's Ironsides. It was his men who carried the day . . . '

'Then that's where he . . . '

Doctor Babbage nodded. 'We cannot be sure — but it seems likely. The Roundheads are taking prisoners — apparently they think they've routed His Majesty well and truly this time. His baggage was captured along with all his personal papers.'

'And the King?'

'He managed to escape with some of his officers.' Babbage looked at me. 'If you're thinking of your father I shouldn't worry too much, my dear. He was always close to the King and it's my belief he would have retreated when the King fled the field. Mayhap he'll come home now.'

I shook my head. 'He won't come home until it's all over. Have you heard where His Majesty went?'

'Not yet — but I imagine he'll try

to reach Oxford and regroup what forces he has left. Don't you worry, my dear, your father's safe enough I'll warrant.'

I thanked him, trying to believe he was right. Yet in my heart I felt something was wrong. Somehow I did not think we would ever see Father again.

Accompanying the doctor to the door, I smiled and waved as he mounted his horse and rode away, hiding my fears. Then I went back into the house and began to walk slowly up the stairs. If the stranger in my bed had been wounded at Naseby, why had he come here to Withington? It was a journey of more than twenty miles, surely he could have found a safe place to stay before this.

When I entered my bedchamber all such thoughts fled from my mind. The stranger was tossing restlessly, his handsome face flushed with fever. He had thrown off the bedcovers in his torment and his body was glistening with sweat. I touched his skin. He was burning hot. I turned away to fetch Bessie, but as I did so his hand closed around my wrist. He opened his eyes, staring straight at me but without seeing me, calling a name aloud I could not quite catch. Something stirred deep within me, an instinct older than time.

I bent over him, smoothing the damp hair from his brow. My action seemed to soothe him and he let go of my wrist. Smiling, I spoke softly to him as I poured cool water into a basin and began to bathe his face and neck. Why should I stand aside when he needed my help? My nursing had brought Prudence through many an illness, and Sarah had told me I had healing hands.

I could not save my grandmother, but she had gone willingly to the arms of her Maker, worn out by pain and the passing years. This was different; I felt it instinctively. The stranger was young and strong — and I found him beautiful as I looked down on his face.

I was conscious of an overwhelming desire to see him smile at me again, and suddenly I knew he would not die. He would not die because I should refuse to let it happen.

2

THE sun was warm on my face as I stood at the window of my bedchamber looking out at the devastation left by the storm of two nights previously. Broken branches from the orchard, leaves and flower heads were strewn carelessly across the courtyard, tossed where they lay by the might of the wind. Before the onset of war the debris would have been cleared away; now we had so few servants they had no time for such chores.

Sighing, I moved away from the window and walked to the bed, looking down at the man's face. His colour was returning and he was resting easier; I believed the fever had broken. Perhaps I could leave him now to carry out the household tasks I had neglected for his sake. Turning to go, I heard a slight sound and halted, going back to the bed.

His eyes were open now and I saw they were the colour of hazels in autumn. As I watched, his lips moved as if he were trying to speak, but no sound came from him. I poured water into a pewter cup, slipping my arm beneath his head to lift him so that he could swallow a few drops. He gulped the cool water greedily but I would not let him have too much. His eyes followed me as I put down the cup and I smiled at him.

'You will be better soon — already the fever is abating and your wound has stopped bleeding.'

'Who are you?' he asked, his voice little more than a croak.

'My name is Anne. I am the granddaughter of Sir John Taverne and you are in his house.'

'Withington . . . '

I was surprised he should know the name of my home. 'Yes, this is Withington House. How did you know that?'

His eyes seemed to take on a guarded

expression, as though he wished to hide something from me, and he answered my question with another. 'How long have I been here?'

'I found you lying at my gate two nights ago . . . '

'Two nights . . . ' I thought I saw alarm in his face. 'So much time wasted . . . ' He tried to rise, felt the pain in his side and fell back against the pillows with a groan. 'My coat? What have you done with my coat?'

I laid a restraining hand on his shoulder. 'Do not fear, sir, I have what you seek safe. I have kept it with me since it fell from your coat and no one has seen it.'

I took the piece of parchment from the bodice of my gown and gave it to him. His fingers closed around it feverishly and I realised it was important to him. He seemed tense, bewildered, unable to gather his thoughts; then his face cleared and I saw he was really looking at me for the first time.

'You helped me,' he said. 'I remember you bending over me — I thought you were a vision of heaven — then you brought me into the house.' He smiled at me, his eyes meeting mine for one heart-stopping second. 'I have been ungracious, mistress; you saved my life and I have not thanked you.'

'It was no more than I would do for any man who needed my help.' Now it was I who sounded ungracious, but if my voice was cool it was only because I was frightened by the way my heart responded to his smile. No man had ever looked at me the way he was doing now.

'You have a right to be angry — but that paper is important.'

'I am not angry.' I smiled at him, resisting the impulse to reach out and stroke his forehead where a lock of fair hair had fallen across it. There was a warmth spreading through my body like melted honey, slow and thick. 'Will you not tell me your name, sir?'

'Jeremy Allenby — captain of His Majesty's Own.'

I nodded. 'Then you were at Naseby with the King.'

'Yes.' His eyes darkened and I saw pain, fear and revulsion flicker across his face. 'They crushed us . . . '

'Would — would you like to tell me about it?'

He stared at me and I saw rejection in his eyes, then his resistance crumbled and the words began to pour out as though he needed release from the horror inside him.

His voice was low and harsh, the words so vividly alive that I saw the field of Naseby as though I had been there. The opposing armies of King and Parliament were drawn up on parallel hills just outside the village. In the clear light of early morning the standards of both sides waved in the breeze, jewel-coloured in the sun which glinted on the iron helmets and breastplates of the Roundheads. And in their little squares, which looked like giant hedgehogs, were the pikemen, closely flanked by the musketeers with their long guns. On the right and left wings were the cavalry under Cromwell and Ireton, faced by Prince Rupert's Cavalry, Lord Astley's Foot and Langdale with the Northern Horse. The King's Own Regiment and Rupert's Bluecoats formed a reserve at the centre.

'We were in a gay mood,' Jeremy said, 'joking amongst ourselves as we looked at the 'Brewer of Huntingdon's' New Model Army. There was not an aristocrat anywhere to be seen. We had heard they'd cast out Essex and Manchester because of some petty quarrels in their ranks and we thought them fools. They looked a motley rabble and we never doubted we should sweep them before us like so much dust!'

His voice had dropped to a whisper and I had to strain to catch his words. He asked for some water and I gave him another drink, sitting on a stool beside the bed as he began his tale again.

'For a time it seemed as though Prince Rupert would break them with a single charge. He drove Ireton's Horse from the field, but instead of returning to renew his attack he continued the chase too long, leaving the scattered Roundheads to rally to their leaders — as it seems they have been trained to do. Cromwell had disciplined his men well . . . '

'What happened then?' I asked. 'Did they come against you?'

He passed a hand across his eyes. 'Astley's Foot attacked their centre. They broke and fled in confusion, leaving their colours on the ground to hide behind Fairfax and his reserves. We thought the day was won and a cheer went through our ranks — but we had reckoned without Cromwell. He is a fearful man . . . ' His eyes had taken on a distant look and I knew he was reliving the events of that day.

'We should have been warned that no

good could come of it,' he whispered wearily. 'We were doomed from the start. His Majesty saw Strafford's ghost the night before the battle — he was warned not to fight . . . '

'But you did fight. Why?'

'Prince Rupert advised the King to give battle.'

I saw that he was weary and I rose intending to leave him to sleep, but even as I moved he began to speak again.

'We should have watched for that man Cromwell. Even while we thought the day was ours he swept down against us. Whalley broke the Northern Horse while Cromwell fell on our flank, throwing the infantry into confusion. When Rupert finally returned he found not victory as he'd supposed but near defeat. His Majesty tried to rally our forces, riding amongst them at great risk to himself, crying out that one last charge might yet save the day — but it was too late. Our ranks were broken, our men demoralised.

The enemy had captured the artillery and all His Majesty's personal baggage. Many of our people were being taken prisoner, and the King and his officers were forced to flee . . . '

His voice trailed away and I saw shame and defeat flicker in his eyes. I knew that Naseby had been a bitter blow to his hopes and those of His Majesty.

'They say the King escaped. Did you ride with him?'

Jeremy moved his head on the pillow. 'No, we had been separated earlier. I was surrounded by a press of pikemen when I saw His Majesty ride away. I cut my way through them and set out to follow him . . . '

'Was that when you were injured?'

He looked at me then, an odd expression in his eyes as though he was not sure what to say. 'No . . . I escaped with — a companion. We rode towards Haselbech, travelling through the gathering darkness for some hours. Then we rested our horses in a hollow close by a wood. It was as we lay there close to exhaustion that we heard the sound of waggon wheels and a party of horsemen. Creeping closer, we saw they were Roundheads and we heard them jesting one to the other — they were talking about some papers captured at Naseby, and we knew they spoke of the King's cabinet . . . '

He was silent for a moment, and I said, 'You were hurt trying to recapture the King's papers?'

His eyes darkened. 'There were many and we were but two — my companion was killed. I managed to escape with this.' His fingers tightened around the paper and his mouth thinned as he suddenly looked at me. 'I know your family is loyal to the Crown, Mistress Taverne. Would you risk your own safety to serve His Majesty?'

I stared at him, a little startled by the fervent glow in his eyes. 'I hate this war which divides our people, sir. If serving His Majesty will bring an end to the bloodshed I am willing to do what I can.'

His eyes went over me as if he were trying to decide whether he could trust me. 'Why do you wear black?' he asked, his brows narrowing in suspicion. 'I had not thought the Tavernes Puritans.'

Anger flared in me. 'You are ungrateful, sir! If I were your enemy you would even now be lying at my gate. My grandmother has but recently passed away — I am in mourning.'

'Your pardon once again, mistress. I should not have doubted your loyalty, but in these troubled times . . . ' He paused, giving me his sweet smile which was calculated to melt harder hearts than mine. 'I beg you will forgive this unworthy wretch.'

I laughed, unable to resist his charm. I doubted many female hearts could withstand a smile from Captain Allenby. I knew then that I would do anything he asked of me, for I wanted to see approval in those hazel eyes.

'I should be the wretch and I did not

forgive you, Captain Allenby. I did not keep a watch by your side all night to see you fret yourself into another fever! What is this service you would have of me?'

He smiled again and I felt my cheeks grow warm. 'How lovely you are, Mistress Taverne, truly a vision of heaven . . . ' he said, and I shook my head at him. ''Tis this I would ask . . . ' He broke off as the door burst open and Bessie came rushing into the room, her breasts heaving as she gasped out:

'The Roundheads are at the door! They are looking for a dangerous spy and mean to search the house.'

A shiver of fear went through me and I felt the colour drain from my face. 'Someone has betrayed us!' I looked anxiously at Jeremy Allenby. 'Can you walk if Bessie helps you?'

'Yes, but . . . '

'Do not stay to question me,' I said, leaning across his body to press a knot in the carved oak panel behind the bed.

'You must hide until the soldiers have gone.'

A section of the wall slid back as he rolled painfully to the side of the bed and was half lifted to the floor by Bessie. I heard his stifled cry of agony as she thrust him through the narrow opening into the dark passage beyond.

'Lean on me, sir, don't fear I shall let you fall,' she said. 'The secret room is small, but there is a bed you can lie on whilst the house is searched.'

Once they had disappeared inside I closed the panelling, hastily pulling a coverlet over the bed. Then I went out of the room and down the stairs, arriving in time to hear voices raised in anger.

'We have heard the traitor we seek is here,' a man was saying. 'And we have Cromwell's authority to search where we will.'

'Cromwell! Who is this man that he commands such obedience! Some petty colonel from Huntingdon with a high conceit of himself!' That was my grandfather's voice. 'None but His Majesty has authority in my house. Begone, scoundrel. Begone before I have you thrown out of my house!'

Even while I silently applauded my grandfather's courage, I was thinking of the wounded man hidden in our secret room. We had little to gain by antagonising these men who had come to search our home and much to lose. Sir John knew nothing of the fugitive sheltering beneath our roof, having locked himself in his rooms refusing to see anyone but Hoddle. It seemed he must have heard the Roundheads arrive and come out to investigate. In other circumstances I should have blessed them for succeeding where I had failed.

'Good-morning, gentlemen,' I said, coming up to them so silently that they were startled and ceased arguing to stare at me.

Their leader, a tall, dark man with a hard face and piercing grey eyes turned to look at me. For a moment our eyes held in seeming conflict, neither of us willing to give way before the other. Then I thought I saw his lips curve slightly and he bowed his head, his hand dropping from the hilt of his sword.

I looked beyond him, seeing two more troopers in the hall and a dozen more crowding at the door. It was clearly useless to resist, for we had only women servants in the house apart from Hoddle, the groom and a stable lad.

I moved a little closer to my grandfather, giving the Roundhead what I hoped was a calm smile. 'You must forgive us if we do not welcome this intrusion, sir — we are a family in mourning. Lady Taverne died two nights ago. My grandfather is overwrought with grief.' I glanced apologetically at Sir John, trying to warn him to listen and not interfere. 'We must submit to this search if it is necessary to prove our innocence, but . . . ' I looked fiercely at the Roundhead's leader. 'But we would ask you to be brief — and that your men behave with respect.'

The man's stern expression did not falter, but he moved his head in assent. 'I am Colonel Lawrence, Mistress Taverne. I much regret this intrusion at such a time; with your permission I shall accompany you on a tour of the upper regions of the house while my men search the kitchens and outhouses.'

Sir John made a movement of denial, but I laid my hand on his arm, the pressure of my fingers conveying a warning. 'Prudence will need you, Grandfather — please.'

The note of appeal in my voice reached him, and perhaps because we had always understood one another so well, he obeyed without question. 'As you wish, Anne,' he said, turning and walking into the parlour.

I watched him go, angry at his humiliation. To be forced to submit to this search was a bitter blow to his pride. I knew that even a few months ago he would have drawn his sword before he allowed the King's enemies into his house, but what could one grieving old man do against so many?

I forced myself to smile at the man who had shamed my grandfather. 'If you will come with me, Colonel Lawrence, I am sure you will soon discover we have no spies in this house.'

'I trust not, Mistress Taverne. Methinks you have too much good sense to harbour the enemies of the State; nevertheless, I must make the search.'

Looking into his eyes at that moment I found it hard to meet his unflinching gaze, aware that I meant to deceive him, to lie and lie again if I must. He was my enemy and yet he was a gentleman, and I believed him a man of principle. I thought he was a man my father would have been glad to call his friend before the onset of the war. And yet now they would kill each other if they met. What was this madness in men's blood that they must always fight to solve their disputes?

He walked at my side, his pot helmet and iron breastplate a silent reminder of the conflict which had torn England apart. His hair was short in the fashion of the Puritans; his features strong and stern. He towered above me, a broadshouldered, powerful soldier, my enemy and a man to be feared. But even as I looked into his eyes I knew my fear was more for Captain Allenby than myself.

Soon it became obvious I had good reason to be afraid, for Colonel Lawrence was very thorough. He opened the livery cupboards, ran his sword beneath beds and peered into blanket chests. I held my breath as we neared my bedchamber, wondering if anything had been left which might give a clue to the identity of its recent occupant.

However, when I opened the door to admit him, I saw Bessie was already there. Almost every gown I owned had been hastily taken from the armoire and spread across the bed in an untidy heap: petticoats, hose and slippers were strewn over the floor and the stool beside the bed.

Bessie curtsied as I entered, pretending to look flustered. 'Oh, Mistress Anne, forgive me. I've searched everywhere for that brooch you lost. I thought it might have caught on one of your gowns, but I can't find it anywhere.'

'I must have lost it out walking,' I replied, relieved. Amongst all the confusion even the eagle-eyed Colonel Lawrence would find it difficult to discover anything amiss.

Indeed, the realisation that he was intruding in my bed chamber seemed to have its effect on him. He glanced into the almost empty armoire, made a perfunctory sweep beneath the bed and left, as though the sight of my petticoats had made him uncomfortable.

I was a little amused by the Colonel's loss of composure. So he was just a man beneath that fierce mask, I thought, with fears and fancies of his own. Suddenly I was not quite so afraid of him.

After allowing him to search several more rooms I paused at the door of Sarah's bedchamber, my hand resting on the heavy iron latch.

'This is where my grandmother lies, sir. I give you my word the man you seek is not within. Will you not leave her to rest in peace?'

Colonel Lawrence studied my face, his eyes narrowing in suspicion and for a moment I thought he would insist on searching the room. Somehow I knew he still believed the man he sought was hidden somewhere in the house, but he was obviously reluctant to enter Sarah's room.

He bowed his head in assent. 'Very well, Mistress Taverne, I will accept your word — for now. I am a patient man and if the Royalist I seek is hiding here I shall find him in the end. But for the moment I will search no further. I shall call my men together and leave you in peace.'

'You are gracious, sir. I thank you with all my heart.' I smiled at him as he turned to leave. 'But there are attics above. Do you not wish to search them, too?'

His piercing eyes seemed to penetrate my mind and I wished I had not spoken, then he laughed. 'If the man I seek was there, Mistress Taverne, you would not ask. Believe me when I say I admire your courage — however misplaced.'

I felt a tingle run down my spine and I knew he was even more dangerous than I had thought — dangerous to Captain Allenby. Wounded and helpless he had only a frail woman to stand between him and his enemies, yet perhaps only a woman could have saved him from this man.

As Colonel Lawrence turned to go once more I asked: 'Why are you searching for this man? What has he done?'

The smile left his face and his eyes became cold. 'He stole something from me. He and his companion killed five of my men. His companion has been dealt with and it is my intention to recover what was taken from me — and to kill him if he still lives.' He looked into my eyes. 'Believe me, Mistress Taverne, I do not mean to let this man escape me.'

I felt sick and my legs were trembling as I gazed into his flinty eyes. He had treated me with consideration so far, but I knew he would show no mercy to his enemies. He must never discover Captain Allenby's whereabouts — for I could not bear it if his smile was lost to me for ever.

'I believe you, sir,' I whispered, 'though I do not know why you tell me this.'

'No?' Colonel Lawrence raised his brows. 'Then you have nothing to fear, mistress. God be with you.'

'And — and with you, sir.'

He smiled at that. Then he made me a bow which would have rivalled a courtier's elegance; and turning, went down the stairs leaving me staring after him in dismay.

★ ★ ★

I stood at the landing window watching as the Roundheads rode away, listening to the jingling of harness and the impatient stamp of horses' hooves. I counted the troopers, half afraid Colonel Lawrence would leave some of them behind to spy on me, but all fourteen of them went with him. I kept a vigil at the window until they were well out of sight, then I breathed a sigh of relief. They had gone for the moment at least!

I felt Colonel Lawrence suspected me, for he was an intelligent man and I might have liked him if he had not been my enemy. His threat before he left was a clear warning, though softly done. Was he playing a game with me, hoping I would fall into a trap?

When I was satisfied they had all gone I went back to my bedchamber. Bessie was stripping the sheets from the bed and she showed me fresh bloodstains on the silken coverlet. My blood ran cold as I thought of what might have happened if the Colonel had seen them; he would not then have left us in peace without tearing the house apart first.

'Captain Allenby's wound must have opened again when we moved him,' Bessie said. 'I saw this when I returned. I could think of no other way to hide it quickly.'

I nodded. 'It was well done, Bessie — but I think the Colonel still suspects Captain Allenby is here somewhere.'

'Aye.' Bessie frowned. 'That one will not be easily fooled. Our guest must bide where he is — next time we may not be so lucky.'

'Yes. I believe the Roundheads may return — but you said Captain

Allenby's wound had opened again. Is he still conscious?'

'Aye, when I left him — though I think the fever may be returning.'

'I must go to him,' I said, anxious at once. I pressed the knot in the carved panelling. 'Do you keep watch and warn me if the troopers return.'

Bessie frowned. 'You should let me tend him — 'tis not fitting for you to spend so much time alone with him.'

'No one need ever know. It is our secret.' I smiled at her, knowing she was my friend despite her grumbling. 'Do not scold me, Bessie, I shall not change my mind.'

She sighed. 'You were ever a lass to have your own way. I'll not waste my breath in arguing with you, child, but take care what you are about — you do not know this man.'

'I know that he needs my help,' I replied quietly. 'What more is there for me to know? I hardly think he will threaten my virtue in his condition.'

Bessie shook her head at me and let

me go, knowing that I would not listen to her. She had been my nurse, friend and maid for too many years to be deceived by the docile face I showed to the world. Too often she had seen the passion flare in me when I was thwarted.

I smiled to myself as I made my way through dusty passages long unused. The secret ways had been built to hide the family priests when the Tavernes were of the Catholic faith; but over the years oppression and expediency had led to our conversion to the Protestant faith. My grandfather was a confirmed Protestant, having decided in his youth he wanted none of Rome. I knew he had been angered by Archbishop Laud's introduction of the new litany into the church, despising the man's love of rich robes and posturing. Like most fair-minded Englishmen, he had been outraged by the cruelty of the High Commission and Star Chamber courts. The brutal punishment meted out to Pryne, Bastwick and Burton matched the worst cruelties of the Spanish Inquisition; these men having been pilloried, whipped and deprived of their ears simply for daring to speak out against this ecclesiastical tyrant.

All this Sir John deplored, for he was an honest, gentle man though inclined to stubbornness and possessed of a fierce temper when 'twas roused. However, the Tavernes had always been loyal to the Crown and when the time came both he and my father had stood firmly for the King.

So I knew my grandfather would approve of my decision to help Captain Allenby; though, like Bessie, he would expect me to leave his nursing to the servants. Indeed, I hardly knew why I was so determined to care for him myself. I only knew his smile had touched some secret yearning deep inside me, and that I could not bear it if he should die.

When I reached the dimly-lit, windowless room deep in the heart of the house, I saw that he was lying on the bed with his eyes closed. He did not move as I approached and I thought he must be sleeping; but when I laid my hand on his forehead, I found it was hot and damp. Bessie had been right, his fever had returned.

As I hovered over him anxiously his eyes opened and he stared at me blankly; then he seemed to recognise me and grow restless. His hand shot out and gripped my wrist.

'You must help me,' he muttered.

'Of course I will help you,' I replied soothingly, wringing out a cloth in a pan of cool water Bessie had left on the table beside his bed. 'You poor man, we should not have moved you, but we had no choice.'

The fever seemed to have taken possession of him again and he began to fling himself about, throwing off the bedcovers and crying out. He was staring at me but I knew he could not see me. He was muttering, strange half sentences I could not understand.

'No . . . ! please don't let him . . . it's

so cold in here . . . let me out . . . let me out . . . you mustn't cry . . . I can't bear it when you cry . . . '

I smoothed the damp hair from his forehead, realising that he was reliving some incident from his past, something I could not hope to understand. I tucked the covers around him again, soothing him as I would my sister when she was sick. Gradually he seemed to respond to the soft words and the touch of my hands. He lay still, his face pale against the pillows.

I sat beside him watching, occasionally bathing his brow, and after a while he opened his eyes again and seemed to know me. I reached out to bathe his face but he thrust my hands away impatiently.

'You must help me,' he said, more clearly this time. 'You must take this to Richard Grantly of Kimbolton.'

He pressed the crumpled parchment into my hands, falling back against the pillows, exhausted. I stared at the paper he had given me, puzzled. What was this document that it worried him so?

'I know the village of Kimbolton, my mother's sister lives close by, but I must tend your wound,' I faltered as he started up again, his eyes bright with feverish anger.

'No! leave me,' he muttered fiercely. 'Take it now.'

I stared at him. Whatever it was this document meant more to him than his own safety. He had begun to toss feverishly once more and I sensed that my presence was bothering him. He wanted me to do as he had asked, to take this paper to someone called Richard Grantly in Kimbolton. I looked at the crumpled parchment. The journey would take me at least three hours, even if I went across country. But my aunt lived a short distance outside the village and I could stay with her for the night; and it was right that I should tell my aunt and uncle of Sarah's death, something which had been overlooked in all the confusion.

I opened the stained paper he had given me, scanning the words written on it, and then I understood why it was so very important to him. What I held in my hand was an authorisation to release certain papers to the bearer, papers belonging to His Majesty which had been captured at Naseby. No wonder Captain Allenby was so concerned! He had risked his life to rescue those papers and with this authorisation there was still a chance they might be recovered before their contents could be made public.

I no longer had a choice. I had to take this authorisation to someone who would know how to use it. I could have no knowledge of what His Majesty's papers contained, but I knew that they were bound to be of value to his enemies. As a subject of the King I must play my small part in this. Besides, Captain Allenby had asked it of me and that meant more to me than I cared to admit. If I did not go he would be disappointed in me.

I went first to Bessie, entrusting to her the care of *my* Cavalier whilst I was gone. She was to leave her other duties and stay constantly by his side. She promised me faithfully she would do all she could for him, and with this I had to be content, though I knew I should not rest in my mind until I returned to Withington.

When I had finished giving Bessie my instructions I went next to my grandfather and told him the whole story. The knowledge that there was a Royalist fugitive in the house seemed to break through his barrier of grief, if only temporarily, restoring some of his hurt pride. He was delighted we had after all outwitted the Roundhead Colonel, and I saw him smile for the first time in weeks. Although he was naturally reluctant for me to endanger my own safety, he agreed that we had no choice. It was our duty to do what we could to assist in the recovery of papers which could harm His Majesty. So he consented to let me go, stipulating only that I should take my groom with me.

'But can we trust him?' I asked, a little doubtful. Will Green was a surly, secretive man who went about his work with a grudging spirit. I had never liked him.

'It is a risk we must take,' Sir John said. 'There may be more Roundheads lurking in the vicinity — or deserters from either side who would not hesitate to attack a lone woman to steal her horse.'

I knew he was right, though I was reluctant to take Will with me. I looked at my grandfather and saw the tiredness in his face. He was already under a terrible strain, I could not subject him to unnecessary worry for my sake. I reached up and kissed his cheek, wishing I could ease his sorrow, and I felt him tremble as he hugged me to him.

'I shall return in the morning,' I

promised. 'In time . . . ' I saw the pain in his eyes and did not add: 'In time for Sarah's funeral.'

'Go with God, child,' he choked, turning away to hide his grief.

I blinked back my own sudden tears; this was not the time for weeping.

I took a hasty leave of Prudence, who could not understand why I must go myself to our aunt. I did not stop to explain; what she did not know she could not confess, and I was afraid Colonel Lawrence might return at any time. I did not trust that man!

Slipping on a long black cloak, the hood pulled up well over my head, I went outside to where the groom was waiting with my chestnut mare. I was also wearing a vizard, partly to protect my face from the sun and wind, but mostly to conceal my identity from any who might be curious.

The mare whinnied as I approached, nuzzling softly against my hand, searching for the tit-bit I always brought her. She was not disappointed for even in my haste I had not neglected to think of her. I stroked her nose, whispering a greeting as the groom came to help me mount.

I hardly glanced at him as he put me up, merely nodding my head in acknowledgement. When the war was over I should employ another man as my groom, for I did not like the way Will stared at me.

I paused for a moment, looking back at the house. Withington was beautiful in the sunlight, its red brick walls and timber frame mellowed by the passing years. Dark green ivy leaves trailed the garden walls, and the musk roses ran riot in the neglected beds. When the war was over I would set gardeners to restore the grounds — when the war was finally over.

'Are you ready to leave?'

Will Green's inquiry recalled me to a sense of urgency.

'Thank you — yes.'

Frowning, I looked at Will's broad back as he rode just ahead of me. He was a silent man and I had seldom seen him smile. Perhaps his surly manner was the reason I disliked him, though in all fairness I had to admit he was a good worker. Since my father took most of our servants with him to fight for the King, Will had done the work of three men in the stables. I knew I should have been grateful to him and I was — but I could not like him.

I wondered about confiding my mission to him. When we reached Kimbolton I should need to make inquiries as to the whereabouts of Richard Grantly; and since Kimbolton Castle was the home of Edward Montague, 2nd Earl of Manchester and until lately the commander of the Parliamentary forces in the east, I thought it might be dangerous to arouse people's suspicions, and I decided against sharing my secret with Will. There had been something in his eyes this morning which made me uneasy — a kind of insolence I had seen before and done my best to crush. When we reached our destination I would think of some excuse to visit the village alone.

There was not a cloud to be seen in the sky; above me the sun shone warmly drying the rain of two nights previously, and the earth was firm beneath my horse's hooves. To one side of us stretched undulating fields with the thatched buildings of our farm in the distance, on the other thick woods teamed with secret, creeping life, and beyond the woods wound the dark brown waters of the river. We passed a shallow pool thick with reeds where lapwing, snipe and black-tailed godwits waded in the mud searching for food. Somewhere I could hear a lark singing as it soared high in the sky, the beauty of its sweet song touching something deep within me.

Away from the house, I could forget my grief for a while. Memories of happier days stirred in my mind as I recalled other journeys. In the past I had often ridden this way with my father. I smiled remembering the day of the otter hunt, when as a small child I had been so proud to be one of the company, enjoying the excitement of following the dogs and the laughter of my father's friends. But my pleasure had turned to tears when the terrified animal was finally caught and I saw it torn to pieces by the hounds. My father had swept me up in his arms, kissing away my fright and teasing me until the pain passed.

I tried to conjure up a picture of him in my mind and was frightened because I could not see his face. I must never forget him! Where was he now? If only he could know how much we needed him . . .

Perhaps because my thoughts were so far away, I did not realise we were being followed until Will shouted and pointed to a party of horsemen approaching fast. Immediately, I recognised them as Roundheads and my first instinct was to flee; but even as I urged my mare to a gallop, Will caught at the reins.

'Let go,' I snapped, angry at his impertinence. 'I am sure we can outpace them.'

'And arouse their suspicions?' Will grunted. 'Nay, Mistress Taverne, let them come up with us. They've searched the house and found nought — speak them fair and they'll let us go on. Colonel Lawrence is a hard man but he'll not harm a woman — no matter if she be harbouring a Royalist spy.'

I stared at him, startled. So Will knew of Captain Allenby's presence in the house. Would he betray me?

He must have read my thoughts, for his thick brows met in a frown and he shook his head. 'Nay, I'll not tell him. I've no love of Roundheads.'

I thanked him, feeling shaken. How many others knew my secret, and for how long could I continue to deceive the Roundhead colonel? I fought hard to control my fear as the troopers rode up to us and I gazed into the steely eyes of their leader.

'May I ask where you are going,

Mistress Taverne?'

'To the village of Kimbolton, Colonel Lawrence.' I bit my lip in chagrin as I realised he had recognised me at once, had probably been waiting and watching for me to leave the house.

'What business have you there?'

The angry colour rose in my cheeks and I was glad of the velvet mask covering my face. I lifted my head haughtily, meeting his challenge. 'I was not aware I needed permission to travel, sir. I go to visit my aunt — to tell her of Lady Taverne's death.'

Colonel Lawrence inclined his head and I saw a gleam of admiration in his eyes. He looked as if he was enjoying himself and the knowledge annoyed me. I was in no mood for playing games.

'Then you will allow me to accompany you, Mistress Taverne. It is dangerous for a woman to travel the roads alone in these perilous times.' He turned in the saddle to bark an order at his men. 'Two of you fall in behind — the rest of you remain at your posts. You know what to do.'

There was an ominous warning in his voice which I guessed was meant for me. He suspected something was afoot, but at this moment he was not quite sure what. I realised he was taking precautions in case I was trying to draw him off while Captain Allenby escaped.

Well, there was no harm in that, Captain Allenby would not be leaving for some time yet; but if the Roundhead colonel believed I was trying to lead him away from Withington, he might simply accompany me to my aunt's house and then depart. It was a nuisance because it meant I must go to Barnwell Hall before seeking out Richard Grantly, but I should just have to change my plans. I would accept Colonel Lawrence's escort and then take my chance to slip away later.

3

FOUR people were seated round the refrectory table in the long dining-parlour of Barnwell Hall — and one of them was my enemy. I was conscious of his eyes watching me throughout supper, his lips curved in a slight smile as though he could see into my mind and read the impatience there. Why, oh, why had Aunt Sophia asked Colonel Lawrence to dine with us?

I glanced at my uncle, feeling a flicker of revulsion as he belched loudly and wiped his mouth on the napkin tucked into the neck of his shirt. Thomas Barnwell seemed to me a coarse, unfeeling man and I had never understood why my aunt had married him. I supposed it was because she had remained unwed until late in life and snatched at what may have been her last chance to marry; for myself I had rather have stayed a spinster.

I could not help feeling sorry for Aunt Sophia despite all the trappings of wealth she displayed on her person. Of what use were satin gowns and fine jewel when she was so obviously unhappy?

My uncle and Colonel Lawrence were discussing the war, the Colonel listening politely as Thomas ranted on. My uncle was wont to complain about anything which affected his profits. Having been for some years a shareholder in the East India Company, he resented the King's persistent granting of monopolies to his courtiers whilst the merchants had to bear the whole cost of defending their ships and the trading posts in Madras and Surat. He had sided with Parliament at the outset, but now he was tired of the war which brought him no profit.

'Damn it, sir, the King's defeated,' he growled, drinking deeply from his solid silver wine cup. ''Tis time a peace was made before the country's ruined.'

Colonel Lawrence betrayed his impatience only by the flicker of a muscle in his cheek. 'Neither I nor my colleagues have any love for this war. We can only pray the King will see reason.'

'This war is not of His Majesty's making; he would gladly end it tomorrow if an honourable settlement could be reached . . . ' my voice trailed off as I saw his eyes spark with anger.

'Honour? If I believed the King would honour his promises I would lay down my sword tomorrow. Unfortunately, I know him to be devious and unworthy of trust.'

'Sir! you are disrespectful,' Aunt Sophia cried, stung to a rare protest. 'His Majesty may sometimes be misguided, but . . . '

'Sophia, be quiet.' Her husband glared at her and she turned pale.

My eyes met Colonel Lawrence's across the table. 'Are you then so certain your cause is just?' I asked. 'Can you tell me the difference between a king who raises taxes for ships and a parliament who takes a poor man's cow to pay for a war against that king? What gives you and men like Oliver Cromwell the right to judge what is best for England?'

'Anne, my dear, you should not.'

I heard Aunt Sophia's shocked protest and knew I had been rude, but I was not sorry for what I had said, merely annoyed with myself for letting him see so plainly where my loyalties lay.

To my surprise he smiled at me. 'To the poor man there is little difference, Mistress Taverne; but we are fighting for our freedom and everyone must bear their share of the cost. For myself I do not presume to sit in judgement, but I have faith in the cause for which we fight. Cromwell is a man of vision and I admire him for his qualities as a soldier. At Marston Moor I saw him rally men who were beaten and turn defeat into victory. When Manchester and Fairfax had all but given up, Cromwell rode against Goring's calvalry though he was wounded.

'And you slaughtered Newcastle's Whitecoats where they stood.'

He met my accusing eyes. 'In war men must die. Do you not think we would have given quarter if they had surrendered?'

'Perhaps.' Something in his eyes stopped me protesting further.

'Now, sir, tell us what you meant by your accusation against the King.' My uncle frowned at me as though warning me I had already said too much. 'Why do you say he cannot be trusted to keep his word?'

Colonel Lawrence was staring moodily into his wine glass as if his thoughts were far away. He raised his eyes then and looked directly at me. 'Certain papers captured at Naseby will prove the King's infamy when they are laid before Parliament.'

My hand trembled on the stem of

my wine cup and I could not look at him. Had I underestimated him? Could he have guessed why I had come to Kimbolton? I was suddenly frightened of him and I wanted to escape his piercing eyes. Pushing back my chair, I stood up and turned to my aunt.

'I am very tired. May I be allowed to retire to my room?'

Aunt Sophia rose and came round the table to join me. 'Of course, my dear. You must be worn out with nursing your grandmother all those weeks.' She took my hands in hers, smiling. 'Come, we shall go upstairs together. You will excuse us, gentlemen?'

Her husband frowned. 'Yes, yes, leave us to our wine. Mayhap we can have a sensible conversation without the foolish prattle of women.'

Sophia flinched as though he had struck her, but made no reply, merely nodding to Colonel Lawrence as she took my arm and drew me from the room. Outside in the passage she picked up a chamberstick to light our way, smiling at me as we walked upstairs together.

'Your uncle has a touch of colic,' she said, her hand trembling on my arm. 'You must not mind him; he will be in a better humour tomorrow.'

'Yes, of course,' I said, squeezing her hand. 'It was kind of you to ask Colonel Lawrence to sup with us, but I wish you hadn't. I cannot like him.'

'Oh dear! I thought it the least I could do after he was good enough to escort you here. Besides, your uncle likes company at his table.'

'It doesn't matter,' I said, seeing she looked upset. 'I suppose he is entitled to his opinions; but he is my father's enemy.'

'Ah yes, dear Saul. You have not heard from him?'

I shook my head. 'Nothing since his last letter.'

Aunt Sophia sighed and looked sad. I knew she was fond of my father and I wondered if I had perhaps solved the mystery of why she had waited so long to marry. Could it be that she had loved Saul Taverne, wedding another when he asked her sister to be his wife? If it was so she had never given any sign of her disappointment, and I knew she and my mother had been very close.

She smiled at me, her eyes misty with memories. 'Saul was ever the King's man. I met him once — His Majesty I mean. It was when the old king was alive and Charles still the Prince of Wales. He was rather a shy young man. He stammered when we were introduced and kissed my hand. I don't believe all the wicked things people say of him — no matter what Thomas thinks!'

There was a note of defiance in her voice and I felt a rush of sympathy for her. Thomas Barnwell could not be an easy man to live with. Impulsively, I kissed her cheek and was startled to see tears in her faded eyes.

'My dearest child,' she said, returning my kiss moistly, 'You know there is always a home here for you and Prudence.'

'Thank you,' I replied, knowing I could never bring myself to live under my uncle's roof.

By now we had reached the bedchamber which was to be mine. I glanced around it as we went in. Like every other room in the house it was richly furnished with carpets and hangings of damask silk. At either side of the room were small carved tables with matching chambersticks of cast silver, and a long padded stool stood at the foot of the four-posted bed. On a side-table by the window was a writing-cabinet cross-banded with silver and the open fireplace was flanked by two chairs with embroidered seats.

It was far more luxurious than my own room at Withington, but it did not have the welcoming warmth of my home. Withington might be shabby but I would not have changed it for my aunt's house.

She moved about the room for a few

moments, checking that everything had been provided for my comfort; then she smiled at me. 'I shall leave you to rest now, my dear. Tomorrow we will take the carriage and return to Withington, though I am not sure your uncle will be able to come with us.'

I thanked her, privately hoping my uncle would discover he had pressing business elsewhere, though I knew myself ungrateful. He was kind enough in his own way, often giving Prudence and myself presents when we were children, but I distrusted him and disliked the touch of his moist hands that always seemed to cling to mine a little too long.

Aunt Sophia kissed me again and wished me a restful night; then she left me and I waited until the sound of her footsteps had died away before I peeped out into the passage. My hopes of slipping away to the village earlier had been thwarted by my aunt's invitation to Colonel Lawrence. Somehow I had to leave the house without his seeing me before it grew too late.

The Colonel had accepted my aunt's invitation with alacrity, and I was certain he had done so only to annoy me. It was as if he was daring me to make a false move, like a cat playing with a mouse, enjoying my attempts to escape. But now he himself was trapped, forced to listen to my uncle ranting on about the war. It was my chance to get away and I knew I must take it. If I waited until the morning I should probably find him at the door ready to ride back to Withington with me. No, if I was to deliver that paper, it had to be now.

Going out into the hallway, I locked my door and put the key in a purse hanging from my girdle. At the far end of the hall a candle flickered in the gloom, but I knew it was too dangerous to go that way: someone might see me. I should have to use the back stairs leading down to the kitchens and the servants' quarters.

My heart was thumping as I crept

down the wooden stairs, trying to tread softly so as not to be heard. If I was discovered I should find it hard to explain why I was wearing my cloak and creeping about in the darkness when I was supposed to be in bed. Below me I could see the dark well of the hall and the glow of rush candles in the kitchen. The servants were taking their evening meal and I could hear the sound of their laughter. The door was open but I thought it unlikely they would notice me in the gloom of the hall.

Trying the latch of the first door I came to, I discovered it was a store room full of jars and pewter pans; the next concealed a flight of stone steps leading down into the pitch black of the cellars. I held my breath as I crept nearer the kitchens. Surely there must be a way out to the back courtyard!

The last door was locked but the key was in its place. I turned it carefully, wincing as it made a scraping sound. I was terrified someone would hear and come to investigate, but no one seemed to notice and I sighed with relief, glad that they were busy with their meal. As the door swung open a rush of cool air touched my face and I knew I had found what I was looking for. Hesitating for a moment, I took the key and locked the door behind me. The risk of a servant discovering its loss was less than that of being shut out all night.

Looking about me I found I was in a small yard at the rear of the house. The grey stone walls were covered with creeping honeysuckle and the scent of the flowers was carried softly on the night air. The sky was already dark but the light from a crescent moon was sufficient for my needs. From here I knew I could find my way through the kitchen gardens to the lane beyond.

It was a long walk from Barnwell Hall to the village, and I had never tried to go there in the dark on foot before. I sighed, wishing I dare saddle my mare or that I had never set out on this mission. Pulling my cloak around me, I scolded myself for being faint-hearted and set off. At least I knew where to find Richard Grantly's house having questioned my aunt earlier. She had obligingly told me exactly how to find the house, believing me when I said Mr Grantly was a friend of my father. Fortunately the house was situated a little outside the village itself and so I would run less risk of being seen.

It was cooler tonight now that the sun had gone, and I regretted the warmth of Aunt Sophia's comfortable bed. Somewhere a late blackbird was warbling his rich, fluty song; and a small furry creature scuttled past me in the gathering dusk, startled by the abrasive churring of a nightjar hidden deep in the wood. I wondered why sounds and smells became so much sharper at night. There was the pungent odour of bear's garlic growing deep and dark in the wettest parts of the wood. It was in these secret places that fairy rings were to be found. When I was a tiny child my nurse had warned me never to venture into a fairy ring, for I should disappear never to be seen again by the human eye. That nurse had so frightened Prudence with her tales of demons and goblins that she had gone running to our mother. The nurse had been dismissed and Bessie had taken charge of us; and though I knew she believed in these tales herself, she never used them to frighten us.

However, it was not of hobgoblins I was thinking as I walked swiftly through the woods. My fears were of a more tangible kind. I was afraid that somehow Colonel Lawrence would discover I had slipped away and would follow me.

The village of Kimbolton nestled lazily amongst softly undulating fields, bordered along the north-east by the River Kym. At its centre was a fortified manor house, and within its walls Queen Katherine of Aragon had been kept a lonely, unhappy prisoner until her death. The sight of the castle always made me shiver, thinking of that unlucky wife locked away because she could not give her husband a son.

In truth I had more reason to shiver at the thought of its grim walls tonight, for it was the home of the Earl of Manchester — the King's enemy! My mind returned to the problem of the Roundhead colonel who still represented a threat to Captain Allenby. If I had not mistaken my man he would return with me to Withington in the morning. We could keep our guest hidden in the secret room whilst he was ill, but he could not stay there for ever. I could only hope Colonel Lawrence would tire of this game he was playing and leave us in peace.

I quickened my pace as I saw the spire of the thirteenth century church. It was not much further now. I hoped this Richard Grantly had not retired for the night.

The house my aunt had described was long and low with a sloping thatched roof and red brick walls. It was nestled close by the church as if sheltering beneath its benign wings. I could see it clearly now and there was a light burning in a downstairs window. Drawing a sigh of relief, I began to run towards it, anxious now to complete my mission.

★ ★ ★

Emerging into the cool night air some minutes later I felt a sense of relief that I had delivered the letter to Richard Grantly, even though he had been reluctant to take it from me. His excuse was that he believed he was already suspected of working secretly for the King, and that he doubted he would be able to recover His Majesty's papers.

'By this time they will be safe at Westminster. Cromwell will not let slip such a chance to strike a blow against the Royalist cause,' he said, frowning as he read the contents of the document I had given him. 'You have had a wasted journey, mistress. The safest thing for us all will be for me to destroy this now and forget you came.'

'Could you not at least try?' I asked.

He mumbled something and I knew he would burn the letter as soon as I had gone. For a moment I was tempted to snatch it from his hand and take it back with me. But what could I do with it then?

'Please do what you can,' I said. 'One man has died and another lies sorely injured because they risked their lives for that authorisation.'

He turned his head aside, saying he would do his best. I knew he was lying and the look I gave him could have left him in little doubt of my feelings as I went to the door, slamming it behind me. My journey had been all for nothing!

I was angry as I began the long walk back to Barnwell Hall, angry and disappointed. My great adventure had ended in a dismal failure. Captain Allenby's faith in Mr Grantly had been misplaced; I could only hope he would not betray us both. I believed he would do so if it was to his advantage; and if he did not know me, a few inquiries would tell him all he needed to know. For a second I considered going back to wrest the evidence from him, when I realised it was probably already too late: there was nothing more I could do.

My anger carried me up the steep rise which led to the woods overlooking the village; and it was not until I had been walking for some time that I heard a slight sound and glanced over my shoulder. I could see no one and thought I must have imagined it. Nevertheless, it gave me an uncomfortable feeling and I started to walk faster. I should be glad to be safely back inside my aunt's house, this night's adventure well behind me.

Suddenly I was conscious of being alone and the darkness became threatening. My heart thumped madly and my mouth went dry with fear. To reach Barnwell Hall I must pass through the woods, and now every sound, every dark shape was menacing. The hairs on the back of my neck prickled and my hands were damp with sweat.

Hearing a noise like the snapping of a twig beneath someone's foot I halted, looking over my shoulder once more. This time I thought I saw a man's shadow slip behind a tree and I was terrified. Someone was following me! It was all I could do not to cry out in alarm, but somehow I forced my panic down and went on walking at the same pace. If whoever it was behind me intended me harm the worst thing I could do was to show fear.

I wiped my clammy hands against my cloak, whispering a prayer as I heard the sounds coming nearer. My pursuer was gaining on me. It was taking every ounce of courage I possessed not to start running. I should never have come on this mad errand. I should have waited for daylight. Oh, God — why hadn't I waited?

Stopping suddenly, I turned to face whoever was following me so relentlessly. I had some foolish idea that maybe if I challenged my pursuer he would just go away. Then, as the shadow came nearer, no longer bothering to hide, I saw him clearly for the first time and I drew a sigh of relief. It was only my groom.

'Will, thank goodness!' I cried as I relaxed and let him catch up with me. 'You scared me for a moment.'

Will made no reply; and as he approached me I saw his face in the moonlight. He looked so strange that I was bewildered, my sense of relief draining away as he just stood and stared at me.

'Will, what is it?' I asked, my voice a harsh whisper as the cold finger of fear moved down my spine. 'Why are you staring at me like that?'

Still he said nothing, just keeping his eyes fixed on me. He seemed a man possessed; his pale face shiny with sweat, eyes burning feverishly in their sockets.

'Are you ill?' I asked, wishing he would stop looking at me so oddly.

'You were afraid of me,' he said, and the words sent shivers, running through me: they seemed to please him so much. 'You *are* afraid of me.'

'No, I am not afraid of you now,' I lied, desperately trying to hide my terror.

'You've never really noticed me until today,' he went on as if I had not spoken. 'But this afternoon you were frightened. I saw it in your eyes. And you are frightened now. I thought you so far above me, a goddess, but you are only a woman.'

'You've been drinking,' I said, making my voice sharp in an effort to bring him to his senses. 'I will overlook it this time provided you stop this nonsense.'

He moved closer to me and I retreated, frightened by the look in his eyes. Something was different about him tonight — something more than the effect of his drinking bout.

'I've wanted you for so long, worshipped you as a pet dog would, but you never saw me.' There was bitterness in his voice and I was shocked. I had never once suspected what was going on in his mind. 'I've tried to cast you out like the demon drink. I've prayed for release from your spells, but you've bewitched me!'

'No!' I was shaking with fear. 'I didn't know.'

'Tonight I'm going to take what you've denied me. Smile for me. I want to see you smile at me.'

'You are mad!' I cried, backing away from him. 'No, don't come near me.'

I held out my hand to ward him off, but I could see he was not listening to me. My words were no more to him than the whispering of the wind in the trees. Some strange force was driving him and he was filled with the sense of his own power. He was either drunk or insane. He spoke of worshipping me, but what I saw in his face was not love. He wanted to hurt me, to humiliate me, to subject me to his vile lusts.

I could hardly believe this was happening to me. This was Will Green, a man I had known as a trusted servant. But no, this creature was not the man I had seen working in my stables: this was a beast from some nightmarish dream!

I knew it would be useless to reason with him. My eyes never leaving his face, I began to back away from him. Somehow I must trick him into letting me go.

'Think what you are doing,' I said. 'If you harm me you will lose your position — mayhap even your life. It is not worth it.'

He ignored my pleas. It was as if he believed himself omnipotent, as if nothing could stop him taking what he so desperately craved. I was no longer the granddaughter of his employer but a vunerable woman. He was determined to possess me, to crush me beneath the savagery of his body.

I gave a moan of terror, unable to hold back my fear. Now I sought to escape, twisting and turning like a cornered animal. My efforts had him grinning, his face a mask of brutish passion. Fascinated, I watched a drop of saliva trickle down his chin as he reached out for me.

I stumbled away from him, screaming. In my panic I did not see the half-buried root of a tree and I caught my foot in it. Immediately, Will's arms closed around me from behind, almost cracking my ribs in the fierceness of his attack. His hands clawed clumsily at my breasts as he tried to rip away the soft material. He forced his mouth over mine, slobbering in his excitement, and I felt sick as I smelt the foul odour of his breath.

I raked his face with my nails, screaming again as he let go of me in surprise. Then he came at me once more, deliberately hurting me now. His fingers bit into my flesh as he forced me backwards to the ground. I gave a desparing cry as he began to fumble with my skirts, feeling the sting of stones scraping my flesh as I fought him. Now he had his hand around my throat, choking me, crushing my resistance. I closed my eyes, faintness washing over me, knowing he was too strong for me.

Suddenly he gave a hoarse cry and the terrible weight was jerked off me. I opened my eyes to see two men locked together in a fearful struggle, rolling over and over on the earth. For a moment I could not move. I lay still, gasping and sobbing hardly able to understand what was happening.

It was only as I rose unsteadily to my feet that I recognised the man who had come to my assistance. It was Colonel Lawrence! My enemy!

Instinct told me to flee while I had the chance, but something stronger kept my feet chained to the ground. I could only stand and watch in horror as the fight veered to and fro, realising quickly that the outcome was not certain. Strong and powerful as he was, Colonel Lawrence had met his match in the burly groom.

In a swordfight I knew the odds would have been in the Roundhead's favour, but this was a test of brute strength. And Will Green seemed to have an unnatural power as though he were possessed of the devil, taking Colonel Lawrence's blows as if they were the futile pawings of a child's fists. He was gradually gaining the advantage. He was going to win!

I gasped as I saw Will's hands tighten round his opponent's throat. His face was lit with an unholy glee as he forced the Roundhead to his knees, slowly squeezing the breath from his body. His eyes glittered insanely and he gave a cry of triumph.

He would kill Colonel Lawrence and then he would turn his attention back to me! All at once I was shocked into action. Looking desperately for something to use as a weapon, I saw a piece of rough stone not far away. I picked it up without really thinking what I was doing and rushed at Will, striking him between his shoulders, hitting him as hard as I could again and again. My blows were sufficient to knock him off balance; and as he swayed on his feet, Colonel Lawrence seized the chance to throw off his hands.

I saw the Colonel's arm come up swiftly and the next moment Will staggered back, clutching at his belly and groaning. He tottered a few steps swaying unsteadily as blood dripped between his fingers, a surprised look in his eyes. Then he gave a hoarse cry and crumpled slowly to the ground, twitching violently for several minutes before he finally lay still.

I stared down at him in horror, feeling the nausea wash over me. Then I looked at Colonel Lawrence, who was holding the bloodstained knife in his hands and was frozen where he stood like a life-sized statue.

'You killed him,' I whispered, my voice harsh with shock. 'You killed him!

My words brought him back to life. He wiped the blade of his dagger on the grass, his expression one of indifference. 'What would you have had me do?' he asked, a slight edge to his voice. 'Perhaps you had preferred it and I let him finish his work?'

I shook my head shivering as the revulsion ran through me. 'No — forgive me. You did what you had to do. Mine is the sin; his blood is on my hands, not yours.'

Colonel Lawrence laughed bitterly. 'What? Will you take the sin on your eternal soul, Mistress Taverne? Spare yourself the agony of eternal damnation, I am well able to bear it. I have killed more men than I can remember. One more will make scant difference.'

'But this was not war.'

'No?' He raised his dark brows. 'Why

are you abroad so late, mistress? What dark and secret business brings you forth at this hour?'

I was silent, recalling that this man was my enemy. He had this night saved me from a terrible fate; he had killed for me! And yet we stood on opposite sides of a great divide.

He smiled as I did not answer. 'A lover's tryst perhaps?' The smile faded from his lips. 'Or was there perhaps some other reason for your journey?'

I stared at him, my heart hammering wildly. 'What mean you, sir?'

'Did you not set out this evening to deliver a certain document to one Richard Grantly?'

I gasped. 'You were spying on me!'

'I followed you from Barnwell Hall.' His mouth hardened. 'Did you really think me such a fool?'

I could feel the colour draining from my face. 'What will you do?'

'That depends on what Mr Grantly does — if he presents that authorisation he will be arrested as a traitor. If he does not . . . '

'Then you will have no proof it was ever in his possession.'

He bowed his head in assent. 'Let us hope Mr Grantly has the good sense to know his cause is lost.'

'The King is not beaten yet!' I raised my head and looked into his eyes defiantly.

'Perhaps not — we shall see.' He smiled a little oddly. 'If I were you I should return to your aunt's house before you are missed.'

I looked at him. In the moonlight his eyes glittered coldly and I felt he was holding back a terrible anger. The scent of gorse and pine came to me on the breeze and I thought I should never smell them again without remembering the horror of this night. I glanced down at Will's body sprawled grotesquely at my feet and shuddered.

'What of him? Should we not tell someone?'

'No.' He was firm and I was unable

to resist the strength of his will. He dominated me with his eyes, forcing me to obey him. 'Say nought of this affair to anyone; your servant will simply disappear.'

'But you were defending yourself. I can swear to it.'

'It was not of myself I was thinking, mistress. Consider what others will say of you. Why were you here at this hour? Why did this man molest you?'

I knew he was right. Opinion in the village was already against me. Few would believe my story. I should be branded as a wanton who had enticed a god-fearing man to step above his station. I should be accused of luring him to his death.

'Why should you care what happens to me?' I asked, looking into his stern face.

A flicker of amusement passed through his eyes. 'Let your vanity answer, Mistress Taverne, for I shall not. Believe it for love of your beautiful eyes if you will.'

His voice was sharp with mockery and I recoiled as though he had struck me. The shame, fear and remorse within me turned to anger. He need not have murdered Will; he could have simply wounded him, rendering him harmless. Life came cheaply to him and he had taken it wantonly.

'Mock me if you will!' I cried furiously. 'You are a cold, heartless man who takes life as if it were not God-given!'

He smiled. 'Berate me if it eases your guilt, mistress, but for your own sake, if not for mine, keep this our secret.'

I stared at him a moment more, hating him; then I gasped and whirled around, running across the fields as though Beelzebub was at my heels.

I did not look back nor did I stop when I heard him call my name.

★ ★ ★

Reaching my bed chamber I locked the door, leaning against it as I fought for breath. I was trembling from head to foot, and sick with shame. Everything had happened so quickly that I had been too shocked to take it all in. Now the full horror of what had happened hit me with a blinding force. I sank to my knees, clasping my hands in supplication.

'God forgive me,' I whispered, 'for I have sinned.'

Mine had not been the hand which struck the death blow, but mine was the guilt and the shame. Even as I prayed for forgiveness, I knew Colonel Lawrence was right: I could never tell anyone the truth. I would have to bear the knowledge of my sin alone.

★ ★ ★

'I'm so bored,' my sister said, her face sulky. 'We never see anyone these days — and you spend half your time shut up with *that* man.'

I heard her complaint but made no answer. It was three weeks now since

Sarah's death and I knew Prudence was growing tired of seeing nothing but long faces. It was my fault. I had neglected her these past weeks.

'I'm sorry, Prue. I haven't felt much like talking lately.' I smiled at her apologetically, forcing myself to listen to what she was saying.

'How is he today?'

'Grandfather? Much the same.'

'I meant *that* man upstairs.'

'Much better I think. The fever has gone and his wound is healing since we applied the poultice of comfrey.'

'Good. Perhaps he will soon be well enough to leave. Then you may have a little time to spare for me.'

I got up and went to put my arms around her shoulders. 'I know I've neglected you, but I wanted to nurse Captain Allenby myself. Bessie has so much to do these days.'

'Especially since Will Green ran off to join the Roundheads!' Prudence looked indignant. 'I vow he was a rogue for going away like that when

119

we needed him. Do you think it was Will told the troopers we have a fugitive here?'

'It might have been,' I replied carefully.

It had generally been accepted that Will's disappearance was due to his desire to join the Parliamentary forces — especially since the Roundheads who had been billeted in the village had suddenly gone away. The stable lad now came forward to say Will had often talked of volunteering.

Aunt Sophia told me she was convinced it was true. Will's horse had disappeared in the night and my aunt claimed he must have stolen it since her servants knew nothing about it.

'I never did trust that man,' she said to me as we rode back to Withington. 'There was always bad blood in Will Green's family.'

I had mumbled some reply, not daring to look at her. I knew the truth. It had taken me an hour that morning to find a way of covering the bruises on my face and neck left by Will's attack. But I had not been able to hide the shadows beneath my eyes.

Aunt Sophia fussed over me in concern. 'You poor child,' she said, patting my hand, 'you have had much to bear these past weeks. Never fret, my dear, I shall stay with you until you are more yourself.'

I thanked her, inwardly wondering how soon I could persuade her to leave. It would be difficult to keep the secret of the fugitive hidden in our secret room from her if she stayed too long at Withington. It was not that I feared she would deliberately betray him, but because she might do so in a careless moment.

However, I need not have worried. Aunt Sophia stayed for five days, leaving hurriedly when an urgent message arrived from Barnwell Hall. She did not want to go, and she wept as she kissed us good-bye.

'Anne, my dear, remember to send word if you need me. You know you are both welcome at Barnwell whenever you like. I only wish you would come back with me now.'

'We cannot leave Grandfather,' I said. 'Perhaps we shall all be able to visit at Christmastide.'

Aunt Sophia brightened. 'Oh yes, we used to have such merry times when your dear mother was alive. Do come, my dears, I love to see your sweet faces.'

We kissed her and she hurried out to her waiting carriage.

I was relieved when she had gone. It had been a strain hiding the secret of Captain Allenby's presence from her. And my conscience was troubled enough without more lies.

I had eased my conscience a little by devoting myself to nursing Captain Allenby, more determined than ever now to save his life. There were many books in Grandfather's library with recipes for the treatment of fever and wounds. I had tried them all in turn until I found one which seemed to help, watching over him night and day as if I could somehow atone for Will's death by exhausting myself.

I might have felt better if I could have spoken to someone about my guilt, but after a time I came to see that keeping silent was my punishment.

When I first returned to Withington I had lived in hourly dread of a visit from Colonel Lawrence, convinced he would arrive and demand to search the house again. But as the weeks passed and he did not come, I began to relax.

Sometimes I wondered at his forbearance, but perhaps he no longer cared what became of *my* Cavalier now that the King's papers had reached London.

When the news of just what the King's cabinet had contained began to trickle through Sir John refused to believe it. I was shocked, too, by what I read in the newsletters.

Their contents had caused a furore when the letters written in His Majesty's own hand were placed before Parliament. It seemed he had intended to bring in the Duke of Lorraine, the French and the Danes to help him. Half the country was up in arms at the suggestion of foreign soldiers on English soil; but this was only a part of his infamy. He had given a solemn promise to the Irish Catholics, offering them full liberty of conscience if they would support him.

The threat of popery was perhaps more terrible to the ordinary Englishman than any other, the memories of Bloody Mary's reign having been passed down the intervening years from father to son. But the Puritans' hatred of Catholicism went far deeper: they detested the cardinals of Rome and despised the base adulation of the Pope who they believed stole God's honours. They wanted a return to the old church; to be rid of all the popish cant which had crept into the English church of late. It was hardly surprisingly they were horrified by the King's seeming determination to follow the path of Rome.

King Charles's letter to his wife concerning the discussions of a treaty at Uxbridge made it plain he had no respect for Parliament and would break any promises he made. 'As to my calling those at London a parliament,' he wrote. 'If there had been two besides myself of the same opinion, I had not done it; and the argument that prevailed with me was that the calling did no wise acknowledge them to be a parliament, upon which construction and condition I did it, and no otherwise.'

Such letters were bound to cause distrust and dismay amongst honourable men. Even the members of Charles's own party were shocked by his complaints of quarrels and jealousy amongst his courtiers. The battle of Naseby had been less damaging to the King's cause than the capture of his cabinet.

Only now did I truly understand why Captain Allenby had been so anxious for me to take the authorisation for the release of the papers to Richard Grantly; and the knowledge of my failure was a bitter thing.

The memory of that night haunted my dreams, causing me to wake suddenly and shiver with fear. Sometimes I almost wished I could speak to the one person who shared my secret. But he was ruthless and cold and I could expect no help from him. I wished that I had never met Colonel Lawrence, but it was impossible to forget him. I should bear the scars of that last meeting on my soul forever.

'Anne, I'm going for a walk. Will you come with me?'

My sister's question recalled my wandering thoughts. I stared at her blankly and she sighed, repeating her request.

'A walk? Yes, I will come with you, Prue. Shall we take that length of black taffety to Mercy? You could have it made up into a new gown.'

Her face brightened at the thought of a new gown. 'Yes, though I wish it could be a different colour.'

I smiled. 'It will not look too bad with a lace falling band; and it is only for a few months. By Christmastide you will be able to wear grey or lilac.'

Prudence slipped her arm through mine. 'Pale lilac would be pretty — yes, that might suit me.' She sighed heavily.

'Are you very unhappy?' I asked, looking at her.

'Yes.' She fiddled with her girdle strings. 'Would you mind very much if I went to stay with Aunt Sophia for a while?'

'Do you want to?' I was surprised. 'You would have to go alone. I could not leave Grandfather.'

Prudence flushed. 'I would rather be with you, but it is so depressing in this house.'

'Yes, I suppose it is.' I knew she did not mean to be selfish, it was just that she couldn't bear to be cooped up in an atmosphere of unhappiness. She was still such a child. 'You must do as you wish, Prue, but you will not be able to go into company yet.'

'No; perhaps I won't go.' Prudence gave an odd laugh. 'Are you ready? I expect I'll feel better for some fresh air.'

'A walk will do us both good, and Mercy will be pleased to see us. The little she earns from making gowns hardly keeps her from starving. I think I'll take her some of the pies Bessie baked this morning.'

Prudence nodded, not looking at me. 'If I did go to Aunt Sophia's you'd hardly miss me — not while you have Captain Allenby to fuss over . . .'

I shook my head at her. 'Don't be silly, Prue. I have merely been anxious for him. I shall not need to spend so much time with him now he is recovering. He means nothing to me personally.'

Yet even as I spoke the words, I knew I was lying. From the first moment I had cared too much for *my* Cavalier. Soon he would be well enough to leave Withington, and I did not know how I should bear it when he went.

4

AS I entered the secret room, Captain Allenby tossed down the book of verse he had been reading. It was bound in vellum and the poems were copied in my own handwriting from books which had been loaned to me. There were also a few of my own poor efforts, and Jeremy Allenby was the first to read them.

He looked at me and I saw the frustration in his eyes before he smiled. He was bored with weeks of being cooped up in this room and impatient to rejoin the King. Every day he grew stronger and I knew it would not be long before he left us.

'You smell wonderful,' he said, his smile sending my heart on a mad race. 'Like a woody lane after a shower of rain.'

I set my tray down on the table beside him, hiding my pleasure in his compliments. 'How are you today?'

'Better now you've come — I thought you had deserted me,' he said, half teasing, half accusing.

'We've had visitors in the house — the parson and his sister. They are both fervent Puritans and come only to plague us since they know we are not. If they guessed you were here they would send the soldiers for you.'

'You say you are not of their faith. What then? You are not a Catholic?' There was an odd note in his voice which puzzled me.

I shook my head. 'No, we are faithful to the Church of England as it was before Archbishop Laud began the move towards Rome. But we are not opposed to beauty in God's house like the Puritans.'

Jeremy's lip curled. 'Puritans — disciples of the Devil! They'd make everyone as miserable as themselves if they could.'

I sighed. 'I know. They've taken all

the joy from the worship of God and made it merely duty — they will take all the joy from out daily lives if they can.' I poured some wine into a cup and handed it to him. 'What are you reading today?'

'Love's Farewell.'

'Drayton. I remember some of it — 'Since there's no help, come let us kiss and part . . . ' How does it go on?'

'Nay I have done, you get no more of me;

And I am glad, yea glad with all my heart,

That thus so cleanly I myself can free;

Shake hands forever, cancel all our vows . . . '

Jeremy quoted a few lines of the poem, and I turned away from the look in his eyes. He seemed almost to be telling me he would be glad to leave. I understood his restlessness, but I was hurt he should be so eager to go.

To cover the surge of emotion inside

me, I made my voice cold. 'Drink your wine. I have mixed herbs with it to help you regain your strength.'

Jeremy pulled a wry face. 'I vow you will poison me yet — what witches' brew have you concocted now?'

'Basil-thyme and bugle can do you no harm, sir,' I replied haughtily. 'Nor betony — but leave the wine if you fear it.'

Jeremy sipped his drink cautiously, a look of pleasant surprise in his eyes. It had a sweet-scented flavour. He drained the cup and gave it back to me, his eyes mocking me. For a moment as our hands touched I thought he meant to kiss me; then he turned away, his voice harsh as he said, 'What news of His Majesty?'

'I have heard that Montrose and his Highlanders have won a splendid victory in Scotland — and there are rumours the King may try to cut his way through to the North to join him.'

Jeremy's eyes glowed. 'Then all is

not yet lost. If His Majesty can join forces with Montrose we may yet come about.' He got to his feet, pacing about the small room like a caged animal. 'Is there any way you can discover where the King is now? I must go to him.'

'You are not well enough yet.'

He shrugged his shoulders. 'A few more days — a week at most. Your potions have cured me, mistress.' He smiled at me suddenly. 'I need to know where His Majesty is, Anne. Will you ask your friend Babbage what he knows of the King's whereabouts, please?'

From the first I had been unable to resist his smile. 'I will do what I can,' I said, picking up my tray and leaving him before he could see the pain in my eyes.

* * *

We were soon to have news of the King in a way we had not expected. The Scottish army under the Earl of Leven marched from the borders through Tamworth and Birmingham into Worcestershire and Herefordshire, taking the King's garrison of Canon-Froom. Charles, learning of the Scots' victory, made a desperate attempt to reach Scotland and Montrose. Finding his way blocked at Hereford, he made a rapid march through Warwickshire and Northamptonshire to Doncaster, hoping to throw off the Scottish army by these tactics. But outmanouvered at every turn, he decided there was no chance of breaking through the Scots' defences.

Therefore in what seemed a spirit of frustration and despair, he made a sudden sweep east to punish those counties which had for so long defied him, knowing that Cromwell and his Ironsides were safely in the west. On 24 August 1645, Charles took Huntingdon by storm, wreaking havoc as he pressed on through Woburn and Dunstable. From there he went to Buckinghamshire and so to Oxford where he received news of yet another brilliant victory for Montrose.

How his heart must have lifted at the news. While men like Montrose remained loyal to him surely all was not yet lost! And God would not desert him in the end, for he had never wavered in the faith he held so dear that he would risk his kingdom for it. We who prayed for his success might sometimes frown at his human failings, but He who knew all things must surely know the heart of His servant. No, all was not yet lost.

★ ★ ★

Doctor Babbington brought the news of the Royalist victory at Huntingdon. The whole district was shocked by the ease of His Majesty's victory, having believed themselves safe from such attack, but with the parliamentary forces split even Cromwell's stronghold was vunerable.

'They say Huntingdon has been devastated,' Babbage said to my grandfather, his voice quivering with indignation. 'My nephew's barn was burned and he had to flee for his life. 'Tis a bad business, sir. A bad business I say.'

'Surely you exaggerate, Babbage.' Sir John frowned, his hands shaking as he poured more wine into the doctor's glass. 'I have heard there was some plundering — but nothing to speak of. Besides, it serves the scoundrels right for turning traitor to His Majesty.'

'Aye, well, no doubt there's truth in what you say, but . . .'

I crept from the room as battle was fairly joined. They would probably shout at each other for a while and end the best of friends. Babbage really did not care so much and he would come round to my grandfather's opinion eventually, as he usually did. They would neither of them notice I had gone.

My heart was heavy as I went upstairs. It was my duty to report the news of the King's progress through our region to Jeremy, and I knew that it would be the signal for him to leave.

His restlessness had increased of late, and even when we sat reading poetry together, his eyes had a distant look in them and I knew Milton's *L'Allegro* was wasted on him. Oh, he liked the poem well enough, though Milton was now a declared opponent of His Majesty, but he was bored with reading.

Since Prudence left Withington to stay with Aunt Sophia, I had spent as much time with him as I could. Often he would tease me, calling me a Puritan because I liked Milton's *Lycidas*, a pastoral elegy which declaimed against the Laudian church. At other times he would call me a witch and claim I had cast my spell on him.

It was as if he deliberately tried to hurt me, as though he wanted to alienate me; then he would give me a smile of such sweetness and beg my pardon so humbly I was forced to laugh and forgive him.

The times I liked best were when we walked together in the gardens late at night when all the household was abed. At first he could walk only slowly, leaning heavily on my arm, but now he was almost back to normal health. I could think of no reason to keep him with me longer.

When I reached the secret room, which he had learned to call his prison, he was lying on the bed staring at the ceiling, an abandoned copy of Shakespeare's *Romeo and Juliet* by his side. His look of frustration lightened as he saw me.

'I vow I thought you had forgotten me,' he said, laughing as my eyes took fire. 'I had vision of lying here alone until I died of starvation.'

It was his usual greeting. 'Ungrateful wretch!' I cried, echoing the laughter I saw in his eyes, my heart flipping when he smiled. 'I have news for you — the King has taken Huntingdon and gone on to Woburn.

Jeremy sat up, the easy laughter

dying from his face. 'He will make his way back to Oxford and I shall join him there — or sooner, on the road.'

It was out at last, that which had lain between us for so long. He was leaving Withington — and me.

'When will you go?' I fought to keep my voice steady.

'Tomorrow night — can you find me a horse?'

'Yes.' I smiled at him, swallowing my own disappointment so as not to spoil his pleasure. 'Sir John has said you may have his bay. I hope you are aware of the honour, sir! Plato is very dear to his heart: he would not let his own son take him to war.'

'I am honoured — and deeply grateful to Sir John. He has given me his clothes, sanctuary — and now Plato. I shall thank him when he visits me later.'

'He has enjoyed having you here. I think it made it easier for him to accept Sarah's death. He told me you were a sensible young man — high praise from my grandfather, let me tell you!'

Jeremy laughed, his eyes glittering. 'I shall miss you, my honey-tongued vixen. Will you miss this wretch who hath plagued you so since the night you were foolish enough to save his worthless life I wonder.'

'A little perhaps.' I struggled to keep my voice cool, though my heart was pounding in my breast.

'Only a little?' Jeremy's voice was low and persuasive. 'Methinks you lie, sweet temptress. You pretend to be so cool — and yet I'll swear there's fire beneath the ice.'

I could not, would not answer him. It was cruel of him to mock me so — now when he was so soon to leave me. I looked into his eyes and then I gasped: that was not mockery I saw there now!

He got up and came towards me; and as he stood a moment in hesitation, I saw a kind of conflict in him. Then he reached out and took me in his arms. I held out from him for a moment, but only a moment; then I threw myself against him, my arms curving up around his neck as his lips came down on mine and the world seemed to spin into nothingness. We were alone in whirling space half way between heaven and hell.

'Jeremy . . . ' I breathed as he released me.

'Anne, my darling. You know I love you. You must know it.'

'No — how could I? You never spoke of love.'

'How could I not love the angel who saved my life?' His eyes caressed me, sending me dizzy with happiness. 'I would adore you for that alone, but you are so lovely and the perfume of your skin haunts me when you are away from me. I lie here thinking of you hour by hour — wanting you.'

'Oh, Jeremy,' I choked, aching with love for him. 'How shall I bear it when you are gone?'

'How shall I bear it, my darling?' He

kissed my brow lightly, teasingly. 'But I must fight for the King while the war continues.'

'And when it is over?'

'I shall come back to you.'

'But if something should happen to you? People die in war.'

He laughed as he heard the terror in my voice. 'I bear a charmed life — you should know that. I should have been dead when you found me.'

I shook my head, seizing the filmy lawn of his shirt and tugging at it in my distress. 'No. I cannot bear to lose you. I love you. I love you . . . '

'And I adore you.' He drew me closer, kissing my nose, then my eyelids and my lips. I clung to him in hopeless abandon, lost to everything but my love for him and my fear that he would leave me. His kisses grew more passionate, and as I looked up at him, I saw hunger in his eyes, a hunger echoed in me.

'Jeremy . . . ' I breathed again, shaken by the fierce longings sweeping through my body.

'I want you,' he said, his eyes glowing with desire. 'I want to make love to you now.'

I could only gaze into his face as he took my hand and led me to the bed. Somewhere a tiny voice in my mind told me this was wrong, but I shut it out. I wanted this as much as Jeremy. I wanted to lie close in his arms, to feel his body burning mine. I wanted to touch him as I had whilst he was ill, but this time I should not need to hide the love I bore him.

'I love you,' he said, reaching up to unpin my hair, his fingers caressing as he spread it out over my shoulders. 'So beautiful! Do not refuse me, my love, we have only tonight.'

'Please, don't say it,' I begged, tears trembling on my lashes.

But he pulled me down with him, and the tears were gone as he began to remove my clothing piece by piece, kissing me and comforting me with words of love. Perhaps because the hours of nursing had broken down all natural barriers I felt no shyness. It was almost inevitable that we should be lovers. I shivered with delight as his gentle hands caressed me and my own hands reached out for him, enjoying the sensation of moving over his lean body. I was a little anxious lest his wound should pain him, but it was I who cried out in pain as he thrust into me: cried, then clung and whimpered with pleasure as he brought me to a new awareness of our love. Afterwards I lay content in his arms, nestling close to him as he stroked my hair and whispered against my ear.

'You're not sorry?'

'No.' I moved my head in denial, kissing the hollow in his throat. 'I'm glad. I did not know it would be like this.'

'Darling. Sweet, precious wench.' He took my face between his hands, looking into my eyes. 'I shall come back to you. I swear it on my mother's grave. I shall come, Anne.'

'I love you.' I lifted my lips to his.

He claimed them with his own, demanding and receiving my surrender. I trembled beneath him as he came to me again, relishing the sweet pain of his possession, wanting nothing but this wild joy which held us both.

★ ★ ★

A pale moon lit the sky as I led the way to the stables and stood watching Jeremy saddle the great bay gelding. I was finding it hard to keep up my pretence of calmness, but I had vowed last night, after he left my bed, that I would not cry when he went. We had been lovers for such a short time but each precious moment was locked for ever in my heart. I would not spoil those memories by begging him to stay.

Grandfather had insisted Jeremy should dine with us in the parlour for his last meal at Withington, declaring that all the servants knew of his presence in the house anyway. He had sat talking with his guest long into the night while I felt each minute as it passed. My body ached for the moment when I could be alone with my lover. It was our last night — the last time I would feel him so close to me that we were as one. It had been dawn when he left my bed to return to the secret room. I had wept then, but I would not cry now.

His horse was ready and patiently waiting. Jeremy drew me into his arms, kissing me gently. 'It will not be for long,' he promised.

'I pray not — for when you return the war will be over.'

'The war will be won!' he said, and I sensed his excitement. He loved me but he was eager to be gone.

'Amen to that.' I smiled up at him. 'You will meet my father then . . . '

I broke off as I saw the strange look on his face. He turned his head aside and I saw his hands clench at his sides. Then he turned to look at me again and I was shocked by the pain in his eyes.

'Forgive me, Anne — I should have told you. I was afraid to tell you.'

'What? I don't understand.' But a chill had entered my heart and I knew what he meant to say even before he began.

'He told me to come to Withington if we were separated — it was as we lay in the wood . . . when we tried to rescue the King's papers. He was killed, Anne . . . Saul, my friend, your father . . . '

Of course. What a fool I had been not to have guessed it before. It was no accident Jeremy had been at my gate. He had battled on through the storm that night because he intended to reach Withington. I remembered now I had thought it odd he should know the name of my home.

'I tried to save him, Anne, but I was wounded — there were too many of them. I couldn't tell you at first and the longer I left it the harder it became.'

He reached out to draw me into his arms but I held him away with shaking hands. 'Anne, forgive me . . . '

'I understand.' My lips were frozen and I found it difficult to frame the words. 'Where shall I find his body?'

'I do not know for certain. It was by a stream perhaps ten miles north of here. My horse went lame some time after I escaped. By that time I hardly knew what I was doing. I began to walk across the fields. I slept for a while and when I woke I could hardly walk. I do not remember how I managed to find Withington; it was like walking through a mist and only the thought of Saul's promise that you would take me in kept me going.'

'No matter — someone will recall the incident. I shall make inquiries. I must discover where he lies buried.' I was holding myself in tightly, afraid I should give way to the tearing grief inside me.

Jeremy looked at me. I saw he was

anxious but I could not find words to reassure him. 'You look so pale. I should have told you sooner. Shall I stay with you tonight?'

I drew a deep, shuddering breath. I longed for him to stay with me, to know the comfort of his strong arms holding me through the dark hours of my grief, but I knew I must not speak the words which would chain him to my side. If I used my pain to keep him with me now he might never forgive me. Another night would only make our parting harder. If he must go it must be now.

'No, you should leave tonight,' I said, my voice unnaturally calm. 'I shall be better in a moment — it is the shock.'

He hesitated, staring at me with a worried frown and I knew he was hating himself for hurting me. He should have told me earlier, not now when I was about to lose him, too. He knew it and the guilt was written on his face.

I tried to smile at him. 'Please go now. I love you.'

'I love you, Anne. I will come back.'

'I know.'

He hesitated a moment longer. If I had asked he would have stayed, but I did not ask. Now I wanted him to leave me. I wanted to be alone with my grief. He climbed slowly into the saddle, easing the great gelding forward, looking back over his shoulder as if waiting for a sign from me.

I gave him none, remaining stationary until he was out of sight. Then I crumpled to the ground, crushed by the agony of my loss.

My father was dead: his body lay in an unmarked grave in an unknown place. My lover was gone, perhaps never to return.

I was alone.

The scent of pine and gorse came to me on the breeze, reminding me of the night I had seen murder done. And I knew this was my punishment.

I was not alone. I had Grandfather and he needed me. He needed me to be strong and calm. I was his only comfort, his constant companion and friend. For his sake I must learn to smile again, to hide the grief which clawed inside me in the lonely hours of the night.

It was when I lay restless in my bed, which had once contained the body of the man I loved, that I found it hardest to cope with my pain.

At first I wondered if I would bear Jeremy's child, but after a time I knew I should not. I suppose it was a relief, for I should have had to go away to have the babe in secret, but I sometimes felt I would have faced the shame for the joy of holding his child in my arms.

I had not yet told Sir John that his son was dead, fearing the blow would be too much for him. He was still grieving for Sarah and the sad news could not make so very much difference. I would wait until he was stronger.

I had confided in Mercy, the one person I could talk to in my loneliness. Mercy had listened, comforting me as best she could. She offered to help in the search for my father's body.

'I have a friend we can trust,' she said. 'A journeyman who travels between here and Northampton plying his trade as a carpenter. I could ask him to make inquiries.'

'You are my one real friend, Mercy. You will never desert me, will you?'

Mercy shook her head. 'You know I will not — but you will never be entirely alone. God is always with you.'

'Is He?' I sighed. 'Sometimes I wonder . . . '

'Anne! You cannot have lost your faith. I know you are grieving, but . . . '

I looked at her. 'What kind of a god allows men to torture one another in his name? The Puritans march into battle singing psalms; the Royalists cry

For God and King as they draw their swords . . . ' I broke off choking as the tears caught in my throat. 'What sense is there in this terrible war?'

The anger had drained out of me, leaving me trembling and empty. I looked at Mercy with haunted eyes, knowing only that I found the pain inside me almost too much to bear.

Mercy drew me to her, holding me until I stopped shaking. 'Hush, my sweeting, I know you did not mean it, and God in His mercy will know it too. He understands your grief and He will heal it in His own way. You've borne too much these past months and borne it bravely. It is not right you should have only an old man for company — you must write to Prudence and tell her to come home.'

I had stopped shaking now. 'No. Prudence will come when she is ready. Besides, I enjoy being with Grandfather. I'm always too busy these days to be bored. Bessie and I have just finished preserving the last of the soft fruit and soon we shall begin pulling the apples for the winter. Next time I come I will bring you a side of pork. Nat Lucas killed a pig for us last week and Bessie has been cutting the meat to hang in the smokehouse.'

Mercy smiled to see my tears had dried. 'You spoil me, Anne. I hardly know how I should have managed without your help. Meat is scarce since Parliament commandered half the livestock in the village for the soldiers. Everything is so expensive — a fat goose two shillings, ducks eightpence each. I had to pay sixpence for a pound of butter and eggs are three a penny. I daren't even ask the price of a cauliflower; you know how expensive vegetables are!'

I frowned. 'Are you finding it hard to manage? I will send the stable lad with some provision from our storehouse.'

Mercy shook her head. 'Oh no, my love, you already do too much for me.'

'Nonsense. You will not let me do

half enough — but you shall have a fat carp from the stewpond this afternoon and two pigeons.'

Mercy protested again, but I could see she was pleased. She took me into her little workroom to show me a gown she was sewing for the wife of a neighbouring gentleman, going out of her way to lift my spirits. I smiled to please her, but there was no joy in my heart. The days stretched endless and empty before me; as endless as the war.

★ ★ ★

Prudence had not come home, though it was late autumn now. The trees were dressed in subtle shades of orange, rust and gentle browns; and the woods abounded with the fruits of elderberry, sloe, wild pear, beechmast and haws. The apples from our orchard had all been picked and laid out in the loft of the storehouse. Sides of bacon hung in the smokehouse, and barrels of salted mutton and new-made cider stood with the other preserves in the cool depths of the pantry.

Bessie and I worked together with the other members of the household in the rush to prepare the stores for the long winter months ahead. Fodder for the animals was scarce this year with the shortage of labour to gather in the hay, and only the breeding ewes and rams would be kept alive until the spring. Two cows for milking, the bull and a few pigs would be fed through the winter, but the rest must be slaughtered and the meat salted down in barrels. Now most of the work was done and we could begin the spinning and weaving which would help to fill the dull, dark days until spring.

Life continued in its usual pattern despite the war. The news came irregularly and these days it was always bad for the Royalists. In early September Prince Rupert had been forced to surrender Bristol to

General Fairfax after a combined attack by Cromwell, Ireton, Weldon and many others — though he had promised His Majesty he would hold it faithfully for four months no matter what.

In surrendering Prince Rupert had hoped to prevent the waste of many lives, believing it was better to march away to fight another day. He was allowed to bring out his cavalry with all honour; the Roundheads even lending him an escort of a thousand muskets to protect him from the local people who had come to hate him for the way his troops had ravaged the countryside. Rupert's pride had suffered a bitter blow that day, and the irony of the situation was that his uncle had been on his way to relieve the siege when news of the surrender reached him.

King Charles was angry and bewildered by the loss of Bristol, flying into a rage and sending his nephew away. Now he determined to make one last effort to join Montrose in Scotland. From Wales he marched to the relief of Chester, which was held by the Roundheads. He rested his cavalry at Rowton Heath, just outside the city, intending to attack the next day; but before he could do so he was himself attacked by General Poyntz.

'The King's army was caught between two forces,' Doctor Babbage said when he brought us the news. 'They fought with skill and honour but six hundred troops were killed and many more captured.'

'The King, man!' my grandfather cried. 'Did the King escape?'

'I believe he got away safely to Denbigh with the remains of his cavalry.'

'Did his officers escape with him?' I asked, my heart aching as I wondered if Jeremy had been killed or injured in the battle.

'I believe those who were closest to him went with him,' Babbage said, looking a little surprised as he saw my flushed face. 'This means that every port is now closed to His Majesty.'

'Then his cause is lost,' Sir John said.

'Maybe not — if what I hear is true. They say Lord Digby advised the King to retire to his castle at Newark while he himself tries to reach Montrose with the remaining cavalry.'

'Pray God he reaches Scotland safely,' Sir John said, his hands clenched into tight fists.

The next few weeks were full of anxious waiting for all those who supported the King. Digby's plan was daring and brave, but full of risk. At first it seemed as if he might succeed when he defeated a small Roundhead force at Doncaster, but then he suffered a reverse at Sherborne, barely managing to escape. Then after all his heroic efforts he reached Scotland to be met with the news of the final disaster: Montrose had been crushed and his Highlanders disbanded. All hope was now gone and Digby took ship for Ireland in the vain search for a new army.

But perhaps even worse than the defeat of Digby's horse was the capture of his portfolio at Sherborne. Documents proving the intention of bringing foreign troops to English soil were found. Letters from the Queen telling of ten thousand Irish troops — and of money from the Pope!

Revelations such as these could only harm the King and raise the conduct of Parliament in the people's eyes. Many who had always supported the King were now ready to condemn him for his treachery.

Even my grandfather had ceased to defend him so fiercely, though he still hoped an honourable settlement would be found now that the war was drawing to a close.

Our good friend Doctor Babbage brought us the news of the fall of Basing House. The Marquis of Winchester, whose home it was, had defended it stoutly for four years; and it was rumoured when it fell it was provisioned to withstand a siege of several years.

'Cromwell used more than five hundred cannon balls to breach its wall,' Babbage told us. 'Over seventy were killed in the final battle. One of the officers found afterwards was a giant of some nine feet high — they measured him as he lay dead. They say that the architect, Inigo Jones, was one of the fugitives sheltering within its walls on the day it fell at last to Cromwell's men.'

'That man Cromwell! It was a bad day for England when he decided not to take his family and leave for the New World. Without him the war might have gone less well for the rebels.'

Babbage nodded his head, agreeing with my grandfather. Basing House had been stripped of furniture, provisions, gold, silver — anything of value. If anything stirred the good doctor to anger it was the destruction of a man's property.

'When they'd stripped it bare they burned the house to the ground,' he said, his cheeks quivering. 'And the soldiers singing psalms all the while — and when the fire was out the people were told to carry away the stones!'

'God's curse on the rogues,' Sir John cried, shaking with fury. 'Is there no shame in these people? Was not victory enough without such destruction?'

'I've heard it was because they found so many popish books there — they called it a nest of idolatry.' Babbage shook his head, his face grave. ''Tis a bad business, my friend. This whole affair has gone beyond the bounds of decency. A man has the right to fight for his beliefs — but that it should come to this!'

The two men shook their heads, looking grave.

I laid down my embroidery, slipping unnoticed from the room. Collecting my cloak I went out of the house, needing to be alone with my thoughts.

It was more than two months since Jeremy left to rejoin the King, and in that time there had been defeat after defeat for the Royalists. Where was Jeremy now? I was terrified he might have been killed, and I regretted the manner of our parting. His wound had barely healed when he left me. What if it had opened again? He might even now be lying dead in some lonely grave, or wounded and dying by the side of the road. How would I ever know if he did not come back? He had told me nothing of his family except that his home was somewhere in Devon.

'Oh, please don't let him be dead,' I prayed aloud. 'I cannot bear it if he dies.'

I shivered, pulling my cloak around me. The trees were bare of leaves now, their branches clawing starkly at a strangely heavy sky. It was cold enough for snow. I quickened my pace for I intended to call at the farm before I went home.

Sally Lucas, the wife of Nat Lucas, tenant of our farm, was recovering from the birth of her fourth child; and I wanted to see her. She had not been well and her face was pale and listless as she opened the door to me. She smiled wanly as she saw me, inviting me in. The large kitchen was redolent with the smells of cooking, babies and dogs. Sally called the huge grey lurcher to heel when it bounded up to me in clumsy delight, nearly knocking me flying. I sat in the one, high-backed chair before the fire and Sally gave me the new baby to nurse while she cut a slice of honey cake and poured a glass of elderberry wine for me.

I ate the cake and drank the wine because I knew it pleased Sally to give them to me, and I admired the new baby because I fell in love with her the moment I saw her fat, pink cheeks and dark eyes.

'She do grow, don't she,' agreed Sally with a satisfied smile. 'Nat snared three brace of wild duck yestermorn, Mistress Anne. I'll send a brace up to the house tomorrow.'

I smiled. 'Thank you. Grandfather

will be pleased; he is partial to roast duck. Is there anything I can do for you before I go?'

Sally shook her head, taking the baby to lay her in the cradle before the fire. 'I can manage most things meself now — and Nat helps me when he can. Though what with the ploughing and the sheep, he's working from dawn till dusk without my hindering him. He was that grateful for all you done for me when I was bad. If ever you need help yourself I hope you know you've only to ask.'

I smiled. 'I liked helping you, Sally — and I enjoy looking after the children.' She came to the door with me. 'Don't stand there and take a chill. I'll come again when I can.'

Sally ignored my warning, remaining in the doorway to wave until I had climbed the hill and disappeared from sight.

As I walked I was remembering the warm smell of the Lucas baby and the feel of its plump little body in my arms.

For a moment I envied Sally. Despite her long illness she was content with her life. Nat was a good husband who did all he could for her.

I wondered when I would have a husband and children of my own. Jeremy had promised to come back when the war was over — but when would it end? And was he still alive? How could I bear it if I never saw him again?

As I entered the drive, I saw a carriage drawn up outside the house. And, as I began to run towards it, a girl got down. She was dressed in a fashionable gown of pale lilac silk with virago sleeves and a bodice cut square and low across the bosom. Her cloak was thrown back negligently regardless of the cool wind as though she wished to show off her pretty clothes. Her light brown hair was dressed in a new style with little bunches of curls at either side of her face and a wispy fringe caressed her forehead.

'Prudence!' I cried as she started to

go into the house.

Prudence hesitated, turned and then came rushing at me, throwing herself into my arms. 'Anne, my dearest, dearest sister,' she cried, hugging me. 'Have you missed me? I've so much to tell you.'

I held her away from me, looking at her expensive silk gown and fashionable hairstyle. I hardly knew my little sister she had changed so much in the three months she'd been away. She had a new air of confidence and her eyes sparkled at me.

I slipped my arm in hers and we went in together. 'You look wonderful, Prue. What have you been doing with yourself?'

Prudence laughed, tossing her head. 'Aunt Sophia took me to London. We stayed there for three weeks and went simply everywhere. I saw the houses of Parliament, the Tower — and the Exchange. Oh, you never saw such a place! It was so crowded with orange-sellers and carriages and children begging or selling singing-birds in cages. And the shops. Why I vow there was nothing one could not buy!'

I smiled. 'I'm glad you enjoyed yourself, Prue, but surely you did not go into company?'

Prudence flushed guiltily. 'Oh, Aunt Sophia said I could provided I told no one I was in mourning. She said I was too young and pretty to waste my time moping at home.'

I frowned. 'I think that was a little unwise of her — supposing someone recognised you? What would they have thought?'

There was a look of defiance in her eyes. 'Don't scold me when I've just come home, Anne. You know how miserable I was before I went to Aunt Sophia's. Besides, we did not meet anyone who knew who I was. All Uncle Thomas's friends are merchants.'

'Then perhaps no harm was done.' I smiled at her. 'I'm not cross with you, dearest, but I should not say too much to Grandfather if I were you. He might mislike the idea of you being seen in company whilst in mourning for Sarah.'

Prudence chewed her lip. 'Then I shall not tell him, for I want him to be pleased with me.' She turned to me, her face glowing. 'Oh, Anne, I'm so happy. I'm in love! He is the son of Sir Robert Harrington and terribly rich — and he has asked me to marry him.'

I stared at her in astonishment. Prudence was only sixteen and had always seemed such a child to me. Somehow I had not expected her to marry for a long time.

'Oh, Prue,' I said, smothering my doubts as I saw her glowing eyes. I thought her too young to wed but I did not want to spoil her pleasure. 'I'm so glad for you! When will you be married?'

'At Christmas if Sir John will allow it.'

'So soon?' I was startled. 'Surely it would be better to wait until the spring — or next Christmas?'

She pouted her lips and I saw mutiny in her eyes. 'Oh don't *you* say I must wait, Anne. I was counting on you to persuade Grandfather. Philip is so impatient I'm afraid he will not wait.'

I shook my head at her. If I judged the matter right it was Prudence who could not wait. Suddenly I remembered the way I had gone so willingly to Jeremy's arms and I flushed. Who was I to sit in judgement on my sister? Besides, I must not be selfish just because I would miss her if she married.

'Well, we'll see,' I promised, laughing as she hugged me in delight. 'I will talk to Grandfather for you; but when shall we meet this young man of yours?'

Prudence smiled, her confidence returning. 'He is waiting to hear from me — then he will come to ask Grandfather for me properly. He is so handsome, Anna. I know you will like him.'

'If he makes you happy I shall love

him for your sake . . . though I shall
miss you.'

'Miss me?' Prudence looked surprised.
'But you will come and stay with
us in London — and we shall visit
Withington sometimes.'

'Yes, of course.'

I smiled and squeezed her arm. I
knew our lives could never be the same
once Prudence was married, but I had
no intention of spoiling her happiness.

'Come on, let's go and tell Grandfather you're home.'

5

AT first Sir John was very angry with Prudence and he would not listen to either her pleas or mine. I knew beneath his anger was a deep hurt that my sister had seemingly so soon forgotten her grandmother; and, after a little, he consented to meet Prudence's young man.

''Tis plain there will be no peace in the house if the wench hath not her own way!' he declared when Prudence fled from the room in tears after a heated argument. 'I vow the girl hath been spoilt by her aunt.'

'Grandmother loved Prudence very dearly, sir,' I said, my eyes pleading with him to listen. 'She would want her to be happy — and it will be six months by Christmas.'

Sir John sighed. 'It seems as yesterday she sat before the fire at her spinning . . . ' A tiny shudder ran through him as if he could hardly bear the burden of his thoughts. 'The Lord giveth and the Lord taketh away. Amen. Very well, Anne, you may tell your sister she hath my permission to write to this young gallant of hers and invite him to stay. If he proves suitable a betrothal may be arranged in the spring.'

'May they not be betrothed at Christmas and wed in the spring, sir? I am feared she may fret herself into a fever if her hopes are denied completely.'

Sir John glared at me angrily; then his brow cleared and he gave an unwilling laugh. 'What, am I not to be master in my own house? You wretched child! I may as well agree at once for you will not let be until I do.'

I smiled and kissed his cheek. 'Thank you, Grandfather. I will go up to her at once.'

Prudence greeted Sir John's concession with a sullen face, but was reconciled to a spring wedding after I pointed out the advantages.

'You may have a small party at Christmastide — and a betrothal is a solemn promise of marriage. Philip is not like to change his mind in so short a space. Besides, it will give you plenty of time to gather your bride clothes.'

Her face brightened and I knew she had accepted Grandfather's decision. When Philip showed himself in favour of a spring wedding and spoke of redecorating apartments for her at his parents' home, her good humour was completely restored.

Philip Harrington came to Withington a sennight after Prudence's return, bearing gifts for his beloved. They were so many and so varied I could not remember the half of them; but I do recall those he gave to Grandfather and me. For Sir John he brought a copy of Sir Walter Raleigh's *History of the World*, a book he assured us was vastly popular in Town; a pair of caddis leather gloves, and a sword with a finely-worked hilt and a jewelled scabbard. He presented me with a fan of painted chicken skin, a length of Flemish lace and a flagon of a heavy musk perfume he vowed was a favourite with Queen Henrietta Maria.

I found him a little serious, pompous even, and I wondered at Prudence's choice. However, he was strikingly handsome, though I thought his face might have been weak without the tiny pointed beard he wore. Since he was obviously besotted with my sister, I was prepared to make allowances; and when Sir John asked me my opinion, I was able to say I liked him well enough.

'He seems a sensible young man — though I do not understand why he has taken no part in the war. I should have thought any man with an ounce of spirit would have wanted to fight for his King,' Grandfather grunted.

When Sir John put the question to him Philip looked a little defensive, but his answer was honest. 'I am my parents' only child, sir. My father is in poor health and my mother begged me to stay at home. And indeed I thought it my duty to abide by her wishes.'

I smiled a little as I heard his reply, knowing he had been warned by Prudence not to tell Grandfather that had he fought he would have declared for Parliament. What Sir John did not know would not hurt him; and I did not feel it my duty to tell him the Harringtons were Puritans.

Sir John could not quarrel with Philip's reasons for taking no part in the fighting, whatever his private opinions might have been on the subject of a young man who chose to remain at home whilst his country was torn apart by civil war. He told me he considered duty was a matter for the individual and no two persons could hope to see it in the same light. He was reasonably content with my sister's choice of a husband, confiding to me that Mr Harrington was steadier in character than he had expected.

'For once in her life Prudence seems

to have acted wisely,' he said, and I knew that was praise indeed.

Mr Harrington returned home to give his parents the glad news; but he stayed away only a short time, arriving at Withington the day before we were due to journey to Barnwell Hall for the Christmas season. He brought more presents for us all and a letter for Prudence from his mother.

When my sister gave me her letter to read, I thought it gracious but cool. However, Philip's father's letter to Sir John was warm and full of generous praise for his son's fiancée. He declared himself eager for the union between our families, apologising because his health would not allow him to travel in this inclement weather, and speaking of his hope of meeting us very soon.

Aunt Sophia was delighted the betrothal was to take place in her house, congratulating herself for bringing the young couple together.

'How happy they look,' she said to me as we stood together in the gallery

178

above the great chamber watching them. ''Tis a shame you could not come to London with us, Anne. We might have found you a husband, too.'

I blushed and shook my head. 'Poor Grandfather, I think he would find it hard to lose both of us at once. Besides, I am not ready to marry yet.'

I turned my head aside as I spoke, feeling guilty. It made me uncomfortable to deceive my aunt, but I could not confess my love for Jeremy. It must remain my secret until he came back to me.

Aunt Sophia was unaware of my thoughts, patting my hand as if to reassure me. Perhaps she believed I was jealous because Prudence was to be married first while I was the elder. She spoke of taking me to London next year, and I knew she was already planning to find me a husband, but I had already decided I would take Jeremy or no one.

However, I was saved from replying

by the arrival of several visitors who had come to toast the season from the wassail bowl. The bowl, brimming with lambswool, a delicious brew of hot ale, spices, sugar, eggs, cream and roasted apples, was passed to each guest in turn and everyone took a sip, wishing each other good health.

The company then retired to the dining-parlour for a supper of roast goose, broiled pigeons, mincemeat tarts and spiced beef, washed down by quantities of homemade wine and followed by cider cakes, apple pies, cheese and a fine ham. Rising from the table at last and replete with all the good food, we gathered in the great chamber once more to sing carols, listen to music and play silly games. For in spite of Thomas Barnwell's leaning towards Parliament, the spirit of Puritanism had not yet banished Christmas from this house.

The talk was most often of the war and how soon it would be over, for few were in any doubt that the end was near. As most of the guests were of the same persuasion as their host, Sir John found their self-satisfied gloating a sore trial and I saw the anger in his eyes; but he did not wish to spoil Prudence's pleasure so he kept a still tongue and the evening passed off without mishap.

So Prudence was betrothed to Philip and the next day we all returned to Withington. Now the preparations for the wedding began in earnest. Philip went home with a long list of requests from his bride-to-be.

Doctor Babbage came to tell us an amusing story he had heard. 'They say Cromwell's men attacked Lord Wentworth's headquarters and found the Royalist officers playing cards,' he said, 'but with great presence of mind the Cavaliers threw the money out of the window into the snow, where it was pounced upon by the Roundhead troopers in a most ungodly manner.'

Sir John laughed. 'I always said they

were a pack of rogues. What happened then?'

'Why, the Royalists escaped, sir — though 'tis said they left their horses behind in the rush.'

We all laughed at Babbage's tale, but in truth we had little to make us smile in these dark days. The tide had turned against the King and recruits were flocking to join the Parliamentary forces. Though Sir Ralph Hopton fought bravely in the deep snow of mid-winter, we all knew the end could not be far off.

The King had left Newark for Oxford once more; and on the 2nd of March it was decided the Prince of Wales should leave England, for his safety could no longer be guaranteed. It was said the young prince protested fiercely at being forced to leave his father's side, but Charles was adamant. His eldest son must be got away out of the clutches of Parliament, even though it broke his heart to part with the boy.

We heard that Hopton had been forced to surrender on the 14th March. Only Oxford itself now remained to be captured, and it was here King Charles resided with his nephews Prince Rupert and Prince Maurice, who had refused to be driven away despite their uncle's displeasure.

Although the war still dragged on, Philip Harrington managed to send Prudence all the articles she had asked him to secure for her in London. The carrier's waggon was loaded with parcels and band-boxes full of exciting fal-lals, besides her wedding gown and bales of rich materials, some of which Mercy was to make up for her.

Prudence's wedding gown had been made by the mantu-maker she patronised when recently in Town. It was fashioned of Isabelle satin richly embroidered with tiny seed pearls, and the full skirts were open down the front to reveal a petticoat of satin covered by Sedan lace.

'You look beautiful,' I said, tears

stinging my eyes when I saw my sister in her wedding dress.

'Thank you, dearest Anne,' Prudence whispered, nervous now her wedding day had finally arrived. 'Wish me luck.'

'Of course I do,' I replied, kissing her. 'But I'm sure you will be happy; Philip loves you.'

'Yes.' Prudence smiled. 'He is taking me down to Kent for a few weeks; then we shall go up to Town. Of course London is not as gay as it was before the war — but I shall enjoy the shops and the theatres.'

'Yes . . . ' I looked at her doubtfully. 'I'm not sure I should want to visit a public theatre.'

'Oh, Anne,' Prudence gave me a superior smile. 'Don't be so prudish. Aunt Sophia took me and it was so exciting.'

I shrugged my shoulders: this was no time for recriminations. Today was a happy occasion. I smiled and picked up the jessamy gloves, which were heavily scented with jasmine and a customary gift for both bride and groom, handing them to her.

'Come, my love, Grandfather is waiting for you. If you delay longer you will be late.'

★ ★ ★

Prudence was married. The wedding breakfast over; the guests long departed. The bride and groom had driven off in Philip's carriage amidst tears, kisses and fond farewells, showered with flower petals and good wishes.

I was alone again with Grandfather. At first the house seemed empty, for I missed my sister and this time the parting went deeper than before. But there would be letters from Prudence to look forward to; and now the weather was fine I could work in my garden.

I began to take more and more interest in the healing properties of my herbs.

I had always used sweet woodruffe for scenting linen and everyone knew that sweet gale keeps midges away if scattered on window ledges; but I had not hitherto realised clary could be beneficial in treating sore eyes or that cinquefoil would ward off evil spirits.

Since I did not believe in witches, I thought some of the recipes funny, but others intrigued me. I decided I would try to learn more from the books I had found when Jeremy was ill. It would give me something to do to fill the lonely hours.

Sometimes I talked to Grandfather of my finds. He had seen the burning of a witch as a young man and never forgotten it.

'She was nothing but a poor, old crone who spent her life in a hovel at the edge of the village, doing what she could to help those who came to her. Then one day a patient died after taking her cure . . . She was shunned after that and when the witch-finder came — it was a cruel death, Anne.'

I accepted my grandfather's judgement on the subject, though I knew Bessie believed in the powers of witches. I would listen to her tales and wonder, but I believed my grandfather.

As a small child I had learned my letters from a hornbook at my mother's knee, but as I grew older Sir John had taken my education upon himself. He possessed an excellent library, for he had always been a man of learning, and he showed me that the path to knowledge lay in the ability to read with an open and inquiring mind.

He had set my mind free from the chains which bound so many women, and perhaps because of this a special relationship had grown between us. He had given me riches beyond material wealth and so now that he relied upon my company so much I was glad to give back a little of what I had received. I did not find it a chore to stroll quietly through the gardens with him, nor to play bowls on the lawns; though I sometimes cheated a little to let him win, for his joints were growing stiffer with the years. And in the evenings when we sat together in the parlour, I knew he sometimes cheated a little to let me beat him at chess.

So life passed happily enough for me, except in the dark hours of the night when I was alone. It was then my grief came to haunt me, grief I was still unable to share with Sir John. His health was precarious and I was afraid to tell him his son was dead.

It seemed the war was finally over. In April the King fled to the Scottish army at Newark, believing they would offer him an honourable treaty and help restore him to his throne. Oxford still held out against the Parliamentary forces, but on 20th June they could do so no longer and surrendered. They were offered generous terms and marched out with banners flying.

I began to hope Jeremy would return soon, and I thought perhaps we might marry next spring. I would not rush my wedding, for I wanted to give Sir John time to accept the idea. He seemed to have recovered some of his old spirit, and he was spending more time with his friends these days, even riding over to see Babbage occasionally or down to the farm to talk with Nat Lucas.

Grandfather had his friends and the ever faithful Hoddle; and I believed Mercy might be willing to leave her cottage to keep house for him. There was really nothing to stand in the way of my own marriage — and I should visit my grandfather as often as I could. Perhaps in time I might persuade him to live with us, or Jeremy to live here at Withington. Sometimes I felt guilty as I dreamed my secret dreams, but there was no true reason why I should. I knew Sir John would want me to marry one day.

Often I was on the point of telling him that father was dead, but my courage always failed at the last moment. He was forever talking of Saul's return now the fighting was over — how could I destroy his hopes? So I delayed and every day it became more impossible to tell him. Besides, though Mercy's friend had made many inquiries, my father's grave could not be found and I clung to the slim hope Jeremy had been wrong. There was a chance my father had merely been wounded. He might be a prisoner. He might come home, riding up to the house any day now.

I decided to wait until Jeremy came back. Then, if there was no mistake, we could tell Grandfather together.

★ ★ ★

There was an autumn chill in the air as I rode into the stables. I had taken a basket of jellies and cordials to Sally Lucas, who was once more with child and feeling poorly. I had found her sitting with her head on her arms weeping bitterly.

'The doctor said there's to be no more babies,' she explained when I asked what was wrong. 'He thinks I'll likely die this time.'

'I'm sure he did not mean it,' I

cried, cursing Babbage for being so insensitive. 'You must simply take good care of yourself.'

Sally glanced up at me, a distant look in her eyes. 'You're a kind lass, but I know what the doctor says is right. I can feel it. 'Tis not that I'm afeared of dying — 'tis Nat and the babes.'

'You are not going to die. Babbage talks a lot of nonsense! Women don't have to die in childbed, you know. We'll get another doctor when the time comes if need be.'

Sally stared at me. 'Will you be here? Will you be with me when the child comes?'

I smiled. 'Yes, if you want me.'

'I'll not mind dying if you're with me.'

'You are not going to die.'

'Nat will have to marry again. He can't manage the farm and the children alone. If he does — you'll see she's kind to my little ones, won't you?'

'Of course — but I shall not let you die. I want you to believe that.'

Sally stared into my eyes, and then I saw a change in her face. At first she looked startled; then an odd look came into her eyes.

'I believe in you,' she said, and her words sent a little chill through me. It was a strange sensation. 'If you say I won't die — I'll believe it.'

'You won't die.'

I smiled at her and turned away. The Lucas's youngest child was crying for attention and I bent to pick her up, rocking her in my arms. When I looked at Sally again she had a peculiar expression on her face, almost as if she thought I was some kind of a prophetess. I felt a little guilty for I had no magical powers to save her, but I knew that if she believed she was doomed she would make no effort to live.

I stayed with her a little longer, helping to feed the baby and tidy the kitchen before I left. Then I rode back to Withington, my thoughts still with Sally.

The new groom came to take my horse and help me down. He was a friendly man with a pretty, young wife who had cheerfully agreed to assist Bessie in the house. Polly's arrival had made it unnecessary for me to work as hard as last year; and now that things were settling down after the war, we had taken on some men from the village to help with the farm. Fields which had lain fallow throughout the troubles were being ploughed once more.

The groom, a Kimbolton man recommended to me by Aunt Sophia, touched his forelock respectfully. 'Beggin' your pardon, Mistress Anne, but my Polly did say as there be a visitor waitin' in the parlour and that I was to tell you as soon as you arrived.'

'A visitor?' I asked, stripping off my tan gloves. 'Did Polly say who it was?'

'No — but she did say as it were a gentleman she'd never seen afore.'

'Thank you, Jed.' I smiled at him.

'Give Lady a rub down, won't you — and an apple.'

'Aye, mistress.' He grinned at me. 'You do spoil that horse — and she do know it! She be listenin' to your every word.'

I laughed and began to walk toward the house, my heart thumping unevenly. Could it be — was it possible my visitor was Jeremy? It was nearly a year since he'd left — surely it must be him!

I knew I looked untidy. My hair was windblown and my long buskins were stained with the mud of the fields, but I could not stay to tidy myself.

I crossed the courtyard and let myself in the side entrance, the excitement mounting inside me. It must be Jeremy. It had to be! I had missed him so very much. I was trembling as I hurried through the hall and into the parlour, halting abruptly as I saw the man standing before the fireplace, his back towards me.

My heart stopped beating for one terrible moment and the colour drained from my face. I recognised him immediately even though I could not see his face. It was not Jeremy: it was a man I had hoped never to meet again. A man whose face I saw in the nightmares which still haunted me now and then. I could smell the scent of gorse and pine; and my hands clenched into tight fists as I fought the urge to run from the room.

'Good-afternoon, Colonel Lawrence. I believe you wanted to see me?'

He heard my voice and seemed to stiffen, turning very slowly to face me; and in that moment I saw a flame in his eyes. He stared at me as a drowning man might a rope tossed to him which fell just out of reach; and the tenseness in him frightened me. Then he spoke and I thought I had imagined that look as his voice became cold.

'Mistress Taverne, I trust you are well?'

'Yes, I thank you, sir.'

'Sir John — and your sister?'

'Both well. My sister is married and lives in London.'

It was ridiculous! We were talking like old acquaintances who had met after a long parting — but we were not friends. I raised my eyes to his, my first shock turning to anger. Why had he come here? How dare he come to this house!

'Why are you here?' I asked, my lips stiff. 'We can have nothing to say to one another — unless you mean to threaten me?'

He looked puzzled. 'Why should I wish to threaten you? I killed your servant, not you.'

'Then why? The war is over — you have not come to search the house this time?'

'Alone and dressed like this? — hardly. I came to see you.'

'To see me — why?'

I looked at him through the mist of rage blinding me. He was dressed in a grey velvet coat and knee breeches, and his shirt was of the finest holland with deep lace cuffs and collar. His boot hose tops were of the same lace, while his hat boasted a fine plume. He had allowed his hair to grow longer, which softened his stern face. He looked vastly different from the soldier I had met a year ago, though I felt it was not just because of his clothes.

I frowned at him, my eyes dark with anger. Did he really imagine that donning fashionable clothes would make me forget who and what he was?

'I came to see how you had fared — and to tell you nothing remains of that night which might harm you.'

'Then I thank you for that, sir.' I felt a pang of remorse. He had saved me from Will's brutal attack, but I could feel no gratitude towards him. He was a murderer! 'Is there more you would say before you go?'

'No . . . ' He picked up his gloves as if to leave, then stopped. 'Why do you hate me so? Is it because of what happened that night, or because

I fought on the side of Parliament?'

'Neither.' I could scarcely bear to look at him.

'Then why?' He sounded bewildered and I forced myself to look at him.

'Do you really not know?' I asked, seeing the answer in his puzzled look. 'So you did not know when you came here — then you are not so heartless as I thought.'

'Know what?'

'You came here seeking a Royalist fugitive. Do you recall what happened to the man who was with him that night he attacked you?'

'Yes, he was killed in the fighting by the river . . . ' His voice trailed away as he heard my gasp of pain. 'Who was he?'

I felt the sting of tears behind my eyes. 'He was my father.'

A muscle jumped in Christian Lawrence's cheek and I saw an odd look in his eyes. 'Your father — then you have good reason to hate me, Mistress Taverne, though mine was not the hand that slayed him. I apologise for this intrusion which must be unwelcome to you.'

I stared at him, wondering at the look in his eyes; but before I could speak, we were both startled by a strangled cry from the doorway. I spun round to see Sir John watching us.

'Grandfather — you heard! I did not mean you to hear it this way . . . '

But he was not listening to me. I might not have been there for all the impression I made on him at that moment. He was staring at Christian Lawrence, his face purple with anger.

'Get out of my house, sir!' he bellowed with rage. 'How dare you come here? Murderer! Traitor! Get out I say.'

For what seemed an endless moment frozen in time, Christian Lawrence stared at my grandfather, his face revealing none of the horror I knew he felt.

'I should not have come — I will go,' he said, turning to look at me as if to beg my understanding.

He made as if to leave but it was already too late: the harm had been done. I cried out in alarm as Sir John began to choke, clutching at the stiff, old-fashioned ruff around his neck. I started to move towards him, crying out: 'Grandfather — oh no!'

Sir John crumpled and pitched face downwards to the floor; but Christian Lawrence was there before I could reach him. He caught my grandfather as he fell, saving him from striking his head against the edge of the buffet. While I hovered frantically at Sir John's side, the Colonel ripped away his tight ruff and opened his shirt.

Grandfather's eyes were rolling upwards and he seemed to be choking on his tongue. His face was turning blue and he was twitching violently. Christian forced open his clenched teeth and put his finger in Sir John's mouth, clearing the obstruction at the back of his throat. Grandfather stopped making the awful gagging noise and the blueness faded from his lips, but his eyes were glazed and he did not know what was happening around him.

'We must get him to his bedchamber,' Christian said, slipping his arms beneath my grandfather and lifting him gently. 'I am feared he hath suffered a seizure. You must send for his physician.'

'His bedchamber is next to that which was my grandmother's,' I said, too shocked to think of defying him. He had taken charge of the situation so swiftly I hardly knew what had happened. I believed his prompt action had saved Sir John from choking to death.

'I remember,' he said, tight-lipped. 'Do you send for the physician while I lay him in his bed.'

'I will send his servant to you — and the groom shall ride for Doctor Babbage . . .'

But he did not stay to listen to my babbling. Already he was climbing the stairs to Sir John's room.

I hurried to the kitchens, and finding

Bessie there, I sent her with a message to the groom. 'He is to ride for Babbage with all speed and if he find him not at home, he is to enquire where the doctor may be found. Tell him not to return without the physician.'

Leaving Bessie I went in search of Hoddle, discovering him emerging from the linen room, his arms full of his master's shirts and ruffs. Hoddle always insisted on washing and starching Sir John's linen himself since he trusted no one else with the delicate task.

It was a measure of his concern that on hearing what had happened, he thrust the freshly laundered garments into my arms and took off with a loping run at surprising speed for a man of his years.

I followed more slowly, depositing the linen in Sir John's closet, knowing I would not be welcome in Grandfather's bedchamber until Hoddle had made him comfortable. The waiting seemed to go on for ever, and I knew I had contributed to his death. I was certain he was dying and I blamed myself. If only I had told him the truth long ago this need never have happened. It was my fault.

I waited, my nerves stretched to breaking point. When Colonel Lawrence came to me at last, I jumped up, clutching at his arm in my anxiety, all anger with him long evaporated.

'How is he?'

'Sir John's servant is a capable man, he will do all that can be done.' He looked at my pale face and I saw pity and concern in his eyes. 'I have no right to offer you sympathy, Mistress Taverne — but I would have you know I hold myself responsible for this.'

'No — it was as much my fault as yours. I knew my father was dead. I should have told him.'

'I will leave you now — my presence can only be a burden to you — but should you need help you can always reach me through Major Rowland in the village of Raunds.'

I nodded, making no reply and he

turned to leave; but as he did so I whispered his name and he turned to look at me. 'Yes?'

'Stay a moment, I pray you.' I was fighting my tears as he waited patiently for me to recover myself. 'I have made inquiries but no one knows where my father's body lies . . . ' I could not go on but he understood my question.

'We had no way of knowing who your father was that day since he carried no papers. I thought it best he should lie with all the others who had given their lives for the cause in which they believed. I had his body taken to the village of Naseby — John Stonham, parson of that parish, will tell you where he lies.'

I closed my eyes, a whisper of thanks on my lips as the tears began to trickle down my cheeks. I was crying now; the tears I had held back so long flowing from me in my grief.

Surprisingly, Christian Lawrence reached out and took me in his arms, holding me against his chest as

I wept, and I was comforted. We had been enemies but for this moment in time we were but two humans sharing our pain.

'Thank you,' I whispered, my eyes closed as I fought to hold back my tears.

When I opened them and looked for him he had gone.

* * *

Sir John was not destined to die just yet. After two days he was able to speak again, though his words sometimes slurred together and he could only talk with slow, deliberate effort. But he could communicate with me, and he recognised me as I sat by his bed throughout the long, weary hours of that winter.

Christmas came and went and there were no celebrations at Withington. Aunt Sophia asked me to stay with her, but I refused. I would not leave my grandfather, but I did open the presents sent to me by Prudence and her husband.

In London, Parliament sat throughout Christmas day, declaring the usual celebrations a popish rite that was sinful in the eyes of the Lord. Christmas, as Sundays, should be spent in prayer and devotion to duty.

As the old year passed away, Sir John began to improve. At first he had not been able to move his right arm or leg, but now the feeling was gradually returning. Hoddle had tended him day and night, caring for the shell of his master with a fierce devotion which refused to give up the fight even after Babbage declared Sir John would rise from his bed no more.

I was sometimes allowed to hold the cup when my grandfather drank the herb tea I brewed for him, or spoon some calves' foot jelly into his mouth; but Hoddle would allow no one to touch Sir John but himself. He had cared for his master since he was a lad of sixteen, and he would do so until the end. I respected his devotion, though it would have helped me if I had been allowed to do more for Grandfather. However, one afternoon some weeks after his attack, he asked me to read to him from one of his favourite books. And when the feeling returned to his limbs, he reached out and took my hand.

The tears ran down my face. 'Forgive me,' I whispered. 'I should have told you sooner.'

'Not . . . your fault . . . ' he managed, each word a terrible effort. 'Did . . . what . . . you thought best. Always were a . . . good girl.'

I held his wrinkled hand, now so painfully thin, carrying it to my cheek. My heart twisted with pain as I saw the gentle forgiveness in his eyes.

'Oh, Grandfather . . . ' I choked.

He smiled at me and the love flowed between us, healing and clean. Then his hand slipped from mine and his eyes closed. The effort had tired him and he drifted into the half sleeping, half waking limbo which was now his world.

'He will rest easier if you leave for a while.'

Hoddle's words were spoken kindly but firmly. I rose obediently. The roles were reversed and the servant was master here. He suffered my visits with great forbearance, but Sir John's needs were of paramount importance — which was as it should be.

'I will come back later.'

'As you wish.'

His tone implied my return was not necessary, and I knew he was right. My vigil at Sir John's bedside possibly brought more comfort to me than him. Sometimes he was pleased to see me there, but more often than not he was unaware of my presence.

I went slowly downstairs, meeting Bessie in the hall. She looked at me and I could see the anxiety in her eyes. Dear Bessie, she worried about me too much.

'There's a letter come from London,'

she said, making her voice cheerful. 'Perhaps Mistress Prudence is coming to stay at last.'

I took the letter eagerly: it was a long time since Prudence had written. I tore it open and began to read.

'My dearest Anne,' she began. 'I was sorry to hear Grandfather is ill. I know you must be anxious, but he is after all an old man and you should not distress yourself too much if he should die.

We went to a party yesterday, but everyone is so dull here these days. They all dress as if they are Puritans and there is simply nothing to do. Philip's mother says I should wear grey or black but I refuse to be bullied. It's bad enough we cannot go to the theatre any more.

The talk in town is that the Scots intend to sell the King to Parliament, but I take no notice of such gossip.

Sir Robert has been poorly again and Lady Harrington has gone with him to the country, which, you may imagine, is a great relief to me. I adore

Sir Robert, but Lady Harrington is a dreadful prude and forever lecturing me. I am glad she has gone so we may please ourselves at last.

Philip continues as devoted as before and always defends me to his mother, but I cannot like her. Philip says we shall have to go down at Easter, but I shall find some excuse to stay in town as long as I can. I am longing to see you. Cannot you leave Grandfather for a while and come up to London to visit with us? Your loving sister, Prudence.'

I sighed and folded the letter. Prudence had not mentioned our father, though I had told her of his death. I had hoped she might make the effort to come to Withington now that the war was over. Grandfather would have been pleased to see her and Philip.

Bessie frowned as she looked at me, and I knew my feelings must have shown in my face. 'She isn't coming then?'

I sighed. 'She wants me to go to her;

she doesn't seem to understand how ill Grandfather is.'

'Or doesn't want to.' Bessie's face was grim. 'Well, why don't you go? 'Twud do you good to get away from this house for a time. Hoddle can manage the master — and mayhap Mistress Mercy would help if you asked her.'

I shook my head. 'No. I know you mean well, Bessie, but I will not desert Grandfather while he's ill; perhaps I'll go when he's better.'

Bessie clicked her tongue but said no more. She knew my mind was set and there was no point in arguing.

 ★ ★ ★

In February 1647 we heard His Majesty had been taken to Holdenby Hall in Northamptonshire, having been given into the hands of Parliament on payment of £400,000.00. These monies were intended to defray the Scots' expenses incurred in coming to Parliament's aid during the war. However, there were many who declared the Scots had sold the King to his enemies.

'The people of Newcastle taunted the Scots as they marched away,' Babbage told me. 'They called them Jews for selling their honour and some of the women threw stones and emptied chamberpots on their heads.'

'You won't tell Grandfather the King is a prisoner?'

Babbage shook his head. 'No, my dear, it would upset him too much. 'Tis a bad business.'

'Is it true that Parliament has forbidden the army to come nearer London than twenty-five miles?' I asked.

'So they say, Mistress Anne. 'Tis whispered they fall out amongst themselves. The army are determined not to disband until they receive all the pay due to them and some say they are talking secretly with His Majesty. The rumour goes that Cromwell himself is in the plot. He is not best pleased with the Presbyterian party who seem as if they would crush all opinion but their own.'

'Do you think there will be more fighting?' I asked.

'Mayhap — who knows what might happen? The apprentices are asking for playdays to replace the holy days which have been declared illegal — 'tis as though a chill wind blows across the land.'

I stared at him: it was not like Babbage to talk so gloomily. 'Pray God it will not be too long before the talking ends and the King comes into his own again.'

He shook his head at me. 'I wish I could think it might all come about, my dear, but 'tis a bad business.'

* * *

It was a warm day in April when Sir John was first able to walk downstairs again, leaning heavily on the faithful

Hoddle's arm. He had now fully recovered the use of his limbs, but his speech was still affected; something which I knew made him angry.

As April passed into May he became strong enough to venture outside for short walks in the garden with me as his sole support. Now he wanted me with him all the time, delighting in my company. I read to him for hours on end, and sometimes we played chess together in the evenings. His brain was as sharp as ever, though it took him a little longer to make his moves, but he still managed to beat me often enough to please us both.

In May, too, Sally Lucas's child was born. Although the labour was long and hard, she gave birth to a tiny boy and survived her ordeal. Throughout the birth she held on to my hands, her eyes looking into mine with such trust I was almost ashamed. I had done little to help her, and it was to Bessie the thanks were due. But Sally seemed to gain strength from my presence and I was glad to do what I could for her.

I had discovered a new mixture of herbs which was said to help restore women to health after childbirth, and I made a large jugful for Sally. Strangely enough she recovered much faster than last time, and she swore it was because of the cure I had given her.

As my grandfather's health improved, my spirits lifted. The carrier brought several lengths of material and I took them to Mercy for her to make into new gowns. For although most were now wearing the dark colours so favoured by the Puritans, I saw no reason why I should wear them as I was no longer in mourning for Sarah.

All this time I continued to hope Jeremy might come riding up to the house one day. There were so many rumours flying around it was difficult to know what was really happening. Some said His Majesty had escaped, others that the army and Cromwell were planning to restore the monarchy providing the King was willing to agree their terms. And I allowed myself to believe my lover was somehow concerned in these plots. If not, why had he not come to me as he promised?

I could not believe he would betray our love, and I refused to consider the possibility of his death. I chose to think that my lover was alive and working secretly for the King: that was why he could not send me a message. He would not write for fear the letter should fall into the wrong hands.

Soon now the quarrel betwixt King and Parliament would be settled, and then Jeremy would come to me.

6

IT was a warm, soft day in early May with scarcely a breeze to stir the blossoms along the hedges. I paused momentarily on the hilltop, looking down on the village below. In the sunshine the buff stone cottages gleamed whitely contrasting with the dark grey of the church. Cowslips and wild hyacinths clustered the common in the centre of the village, and by the pond the fronds of the willow tree were barely moving.

I breathed deeply of the scented air, something deep within me responding to the stillness of the afternoon. It had a dreamlike quality which touched my soul, making me achingly aware of the beauty all around me. Loneliness moved in me and I felt a strange sadness. It was a bittersweet sensation I could not even explain to myself.

Perhaps I spent too much time alone — dreaming of the lover I had not seen in so many, many months. Perhaps dreams were all that I should ever have.

In the village no one was stirring as I passed, but in the churchyard a brightly-speckled thrush hopped between the mossy gravestones collecting food for its young, while overhead on the branch of a beech tree a blackbird piped a warning. Seeing the mother thrush chase her short-tailed, squabby fledgling beneath the hedge for safety, I smiled to myself as I continued to Sarah's grave. I knelt beside it on the dry earth, pulling at the fresh crop of weeds which had grown since my last visit and laying the flowers I had gathered beneath the headstone.

I sat there in quiet reflection some few moments, feeling close to Sarah as I always did on these visits, hearing her voice in my mind, almost as if she understood my loneliness and my need.

It was almost two years since my grandmother's death, but I still missed her very much; more perhaps than either my mother or my father, though I had loved them both dearly; but in the early days of my childhood they had been often from home, for my father had ever served the King most faithfully. It was Sarah and my grandfather who cared for us when they were away, and though I had looked forward with great eagerness to my parents' visits, it was to Sarah I had turned in times of need.

I saved some flowers for my mother's grave, pausing to tidy it and wishing my father lay beside her as I felt he would have wished. It was one of my deepest regrets that he was buried so far from Withington. I had journeyed to visit his grave once with Grandfather, but he had been buried with many others and we could not be sure just where he lay.

Sighing, I rose to my feet and brushed away the debris clinging to my skirts, pulling my shawl over my shoulders as I prepared to leave. It was then I had the strangest sensation, as though someone was watching me, not in a casual manner, but with an intensity which had somehow communicated itself to me. Glancing round the churchyard I could see no one, yet I was sure I was observed. A slight movement caught my eye and the thrush flew from beneath the bushes into the tree, her wings beating loudly in the still afternoon. Something had disturbed her, too.

I frowned. This was not the first time I had felt someone was spying on me when I visited the graveyard. It had happened on several occasions recently, but I had never managed to discover who the secret watcher was. If there was someone observing me they were at great pains to conceal their identity. Taking one last look around the quiet cemetry I shrugged; mayhap it was my imagination. Anyway, it was time I was leaving now. It was a long walk home and I had spent all afternoon gathering the wild flowers for Sarah's and my mother's graves.

I left the churchyard and passed by the church itself, catching sight of a flash of black as someone disappeared inside. So there had been someone in the cemetry! I wondered if it was Parson Croxley, but doubted that he would be content to watch and not seize the chance to lecture me. Hesitating by the cool porch I considered going in to investigate and find out just who was so interested in my movements; then I shook my head, laughing at myself and my morbid fancies. I was a young woman and I had seen too much of death and sickness. I was letting an unimportant incident upset me for nothing. What did it matter who had been watching me?

I went beneath the wooden arch of the lychgate to the green beyond, pausing to allow a muck-cart pulled by two slow oxen to pass before crossing the road. I let my eyes travel up the long road which wound through the village and on up the hill to Withington, resisting the inclination to cross the meadow and linger by the river a while. Grandfather would be wondering where I was.

'Mistress Taverne, tarry a moment I prithee!'

Hearing Croxley's voice I sighed and wondered if I dared walk on pretending I hadn't heard, but then in a moment I knew I could not if only for politeness' sake. Turning, I saw his thin, black-gowned figure emerge from his cottage a few yards away. It had not been our parson who watched me and fled into the church rather than face me.

I waited for him to catch up with me, schooling my lips to a smile of welcome despite my instinctive dislike of him.

'Good-afternoon, sir.'

I knew Parson Croxley to be a fervent Puritan, rigorously applying the decrees of the new order. I had observed the removal of the altar rails and the beautiful old silver cross which had always seemed to me to shine like a beacon of hope when touched by the sun's rays. I had waited in vain for the joyous sound of bells on Sunday morning, and I had made my silent protest by staying at home.

I knew that I was about to be lectured for my sins; for not content with defacing God's house and subjecting his parishioners to harsh sermons, Croxley was determined to rule our lives if he could. There were to be no more games on Sunday afternoons, for such frivolities led to drinking and the abuse of the Lord's Day. Only last week Croxley had forbidden the ancient custom of going a-maying, declaring from his pulpit, it was a heathen rite and sinful. He had ordered the maypole to be cut down from the village green, ending his long sermon by a fiery denunciation of women's vanity.

Bessie had returned to Withington full of righteous anger. 'The man thinks he's the Squire it seems!' she snorted.

'Giving his orders as though he'd a right to.'

'Perhaps he has,' I sighed. 'We must all obey our new masters.' But I thought that if my grandfather had been younger and stronger he would have driven Croxley from the living.

Croxley doffed his tall hat to me. 'May I walk with you for a little, Mistress Taverne?' he asked, his pale lips lifting back from his teeth in what he meant for a smile. ''Tis my intention to visit Sir John.'

I smothered a sigh. I could not refuse for courtesy's sake, but now I would be forced to accept his company for the whole of the walk back to Withington. He would no doubt give me one of his dull sermons, though I might be spared his criticism since I was wearing a simple grey gown, my hair covered by a lace cap.

'You are welcome to walk with me, sir,' I lied. 'And how is Mistress Croxley?'

'Well enough, I thank you — though

she still has a cough.'

'I'm sorry to hear that,' I said and meant it. I paused momentarily, then: 'I believe a cure made from coltsfoot might ease your sister. Will you allow me to give you something for her?'

Croxley frowned. ''Tis kind of you, Mistress Taverne, but the Lord will provide. Mistress Croxley must pray a little more devoutly and trust in His mercy.'

I did not repeat my offer of help, though I could have screamed at his unfeeling attitude. Although I had never found his sister a pleasant companion, I was truly sorry for her. I should be sorry for any woman who was forced to live in this man's house. Mistress Croxley was of a similar disposition to her brother, smiling only on rare occasions; but I thought perhaps she had little to make her smile under the roof of such a stern disciplinarian.

I believed he was as stubborn as he was fanatical, believing himself one of the 'Chosen'. When he led his congregation in prayer I saw no love or humility in him; it was as though he felt himself able to talk to God as an equal, and it was only we, his sinful congregation, who must fear the Lord's wrath in our wickedness. *He* had seen the glorious truth and *he* had been saved! It was his privilege and his duty to guide the poor sinners he saw all around him, knowing that only *he* stood between us and eternal damnation. I sometimes wondered if *he* considered his own pride a sin, but it seemed he did not.

He glanced at me, a fanatical gleam in his eyes. 'It has come to my notice that you have been absent from church for several weeks now, Mistress Taverne,' he said, his voice rising to the fervent pitch he normally kept for his sermons. 'Since I believe you a devout and good woman at heart, it behoves me to set you once more upon the path to salvation.'

I sighed, biting back the angry retort

which sprang to my lips. 'I have always thought God's house should be a place of joy, sir. I am shocked and appalled by what you have done to our beautiful church. I cannot believe that God was offended by beauty in His house.'

Croxley's race took on the injured expression of a martyr. 'Mistress Taverne, beware I beg you. The Lord be praised! Obviously His hand was in this meeting today. Your soul is in peril — but fear not that I shall allow you to fall into the Devil's trap. I shall save you from the folly of your own nature.'

Now Croxley was really smiling, well pleased with himself and the world. I knew that in his opinion women were creatures of sin, but he seemed to consider my soul worth the saving. I sighed, knowing that I should have to take my place in church next week, for he would give me no peace unless I did so.

★ ★ ★

Towards the end of May a letter came for me from Philip Harrington. Surprised that he should write to me rather than Sir John, I felt a little alarmed, tearing it open and scanning the contents.

His stilted message began: 'Mistress Anne, I pray you will forgive me if I venture to write to you of the health of your sister, my wife, which hath lately given her husband much cause for concern. It is my duty to inform you that we have recently retired to Brooklands, Sir Robert's country estate; the reason for our removal from Town being that Mrs Harrington is in a delicate condition. The child is expected in October, but our physician doubts she will carry the babe full term. She is in a high state of nerves, and I feel it might benefit her if you were to come to her, as she sincerely wishes for such a visit. My messenger will wait for your reply; and should you choose to oblige your sister, I shall send a carriage for you. Ever your respectful brother-in-law, Philip Harrington.'

I considered the letter for over half an hour, reading it several times before taking it to my grandfather.

He looked into my face and saw the anxiety there. 'You must go to her,' he said, his voice firm and decisive. 'Hoddle will look after me.'

'Are you sure? Prudence may just be in one of her moods.'

He shook his head. 'She needs you. I am quite well, my dear. Besides, it will do you good to visit with your sister.'

I hesitated, knowing how much he relied on me, but I wanted to go and he understood my need.

'Then I will go to her.' I smiled at him, loving him more because he released me so willingly. 'I shall reply to Philip's letter at once.'

★ ★ ★

Brooklands was a modern house built only ten years previously with the new wealth Sir Robert had acquired. Of fine proportions, it had murals painted on the walls and plastered ceilings with intricate designs of swags and fruits. Hangings of damask silk framed the leaded windows, which were larger than those at Withington and let in more light. The portraits of the Harrington family adorned the grand salon, an impressive room some sixty-eight feet in length.

A portrait of Prudence painted soon after her marriage was displayed at one side of the large fireplace; and it was this she brought me to see shortly after I arrived.

'It was painted in the style of Van Dyck — though of course it cannot compare with the Master's work. Philip is not truly satisfied with it and he means to commission Pieter van der Fraes to paint another when the child is born.' Prudence sighed heavily and looked at me. 'Do you like it?'

I studied the picture for a while, then shook my head. 'If I am truthful — no, I do not care for it, Prue.

He's made you look too proud — and there's something wrong with the set of your eyes. Who is this Pieter van der Fraes?'[1]

Prudence shrugged, losing interest. 'Oh, just another Dutch artist I suppose. Philip thinks highly of his work. He has worked on commissions for the King I believe.' She sighed again and pressed her hand to the middle of her back. 'Shall we go back to my apartments?'

'As you wish.' I glanced at her face, vaguely troubled by her look of discontent. She was restless and there was a difference in her I could not place. 'Are you tired, my dearest?'

Prudence shook her head, giving me an odd, little smile. 'No, I am well enough I suppose — but we cannot talk here. She may come in at any moment!'

---

[1] later Sir Peter Lely.

I frowned, needing no one to tell me who *she* was. In the short time I had been at Brooklands I had already become very much aware of the antagonism between Lady Harrington and my sister. Whenever they met there was an air of tension, though they seemed to have a mutual agreement not to quarrel openly in front of Philip. I was fairly sure it was this uneasiness which was causing Prudence's moods, for she was in good health and had never looked prettier — apart from the sulky downturn of her mouth. Her hair had a lovely sheen and her cheeks were pink and nicely rounded, though there was a strange expression in her eyes sometimes which caused me concern. For though my sister had always been prone to moods I had never seen her quite like this before.

I slipped my arm around her waist as we walked back to her apartments and she smiled at me, seeming for a moment more like the Prue I loved so dearly.

Her apartments were luxurious, obviously those of a loved wife whose husband spared no expense to please her. Philip had had them decorated specially for her in shades of pink, crimson and deep cream. The half-tester bed was carved with vines and acanthus leaves, and hung with damask silk. The panelled walls were of light oak inlaid with yellow box and white holly in floral patterns. A rich Persian carpet covered the centre of the floor, and two handsome mule chests stood at either side of the door. The table beside her bed was littered with gold and silver trinkets, jumbled together with a feather fan, a discarded glove and a gauze scarf.

Prudence picked up an ivory comb, jabbing at the already perfectly-arranged ringlets clustering beneath her lace caul, the corners of her mouth drooping as she glanced at her reflection in a small handmirror.

'I look old!' she declared. 'How I wish I were you, Anne. I vow you have no notion of the trials of marriage. It is much better to be unwed like you.'

I laughed despite the tiny pain her artless remark had caused me. She could not know how desperately I longed for the return of the man I loved, nor just how much I wanted all those things she seemingly despised.

'I hope to marry one day. I am still only two and twenty, you know.'

Colour crept into Prudence's cheeks as she realised what she'd said. 'Oh, I'm so sorry, Anne. I didn't mean to be unkind. I just supposed you would consider it your duty to stay at home with Grandfather — and I wish I had stayed with you!'

I stared at her in surprise. 'What is wrong, Prue? I thought you were so happy with Philip. He's not unkind to you?'

Prudence sat down on a padded stool beside me, pulling at the stiff material of her gown nervously. 'I suppose he is kind in his way, Anne; he gives me everything I want, but . . . ' She sighed and I saw that sulky expression in her eyes again. 'I know I ought not to complain. It's just that I'm so tired of looking like this!'

'But you look beautiful, Prue. No, really you do!' I laughed at her, trying to lift her mood of depression. 'This is always a difficult time for a woman, but it will soon be over and you will have a child to cuddle. Surely you want your baby?'

Prudence pulled a wry face at me. 'Not if it means being ill and uncomfortable all the time. Do you remember how sick mother used to be? Well, I have been just the same . . . '

'But that stage soon passes.' I thought I saw a flash of fear in Prudence's eyes, and suddenly I believed I understood what was behind her peevishness. 'Mother was too old to have another child, Prue, especially after so many miscarriages, but she wanted to give our father a son so badly. She knew it might be dangerous that last time.'

Prudence bit her lip. 'So many women die in childbirth. I'm only eighteen. I don't want to die. I'm afraid of dying, Anne.'

'Why should you die?' I reached forward and took both her hands in mine, looking into her face. 'You are young and strong, Prue. You will have several children and live to see them grow.'

'No.' Prudence released her hands from mine and walked away to fiddle with the trinkets on her bedside table. 'I won't go through this again. If I live I shall never have another child — no matter what anyone says!'

'You will change your mind when you hold your baby in your arms.' I stood up and went to put my hand on her shoulder. 'You must not let your fears spoil your life, Prue.'

She turned to face me, her eyes glittering with defiance, hard and brilliant. 'You are as bad as Lady Harrington! You think I'm silly and spoiled and making a fuss about nothing — and I thought you cared for me!'

'I do, my love, you know that.' I shook my head at her, not understanding this new Prudence. Always she had been timid and fearful, but always wanting comfort and willing to accept it. 'I cannot agree with you over this, Prue, but I do understand how you feel. You remember Mrs Lucas from the farm? Well, she was frightened last time she gave birth, too, but she lived and so will you. I am quite sure of that, my dearest.'

Suddenly tears welled up in her lovely eyes and she flung herself into my arms, clinging to me desperately. 'I don't want to die, Anne!'

I held her close as she wept, stroking her soft hair and whispering words of comfort as I had so often in the past; and gradually I felt the shuddering grow less.

'You won't die, my love. I promise you.'

She drew back and looked at me.

'I'm afraid, Anne. You'll think I'm silly but . . . '

'But what, Prue?'

'I know I'm going to die young. I saw myself in a dream . . . my hair was spread out around me as though I was floating . . . and my skin was so white . . . I was dead . . . '

My lips moved to deny her but could not speak, for I, too, was seeing her vision. The picture of her lying dead upon the ground flashed into my mind, chilling me with its clarity. Her long hair was straggling upon her shoulders and her face was as white as the ground upon which she lay. Then I saw myself reach out to her, but even as I did so the picture faded and was gone.

'You won't die in childbirth, Prue,' I said. Then I made myself smile at her. 'What a foolish child you are. Shall we go for a walk in the gardens now? The fresh air will do us both good . . . '

She gave me a shy smile. 'I suppose it's silly to be frightened by a dream, isn't it? I'm glad you've come, Anne.

I feel better now I've told you.'

I took her arm, drawing her to the closet to find her cloak and teasing her. But the vision in my mind had been too real for me to forget it easily. I knew it would haunt me for some time.

★ ★ ★

It was the last night of my visit to Brooklands. Tomorrow I was to return home in Philip's carriage. Since our talk Prudence had improved markedly and I felt it was time I left.

During my visit only the local parson and some of Sir Robert's oldest friends had been invited to sup with us, but tonight the Harringtons were having a large party. Instead of retiring to Lady Harrington's closet after dinner as we usually did we would gather in the great hall; though there would be no music or dancing as Lady Harrington did not approve of such junketing.

I spent some while deciding what

gown to wear that evening, settling at last on a pale yellow satin dress. It had a wide skirt open at the front over a petticoat of cream silk embroidered with gold thread, and the sleeves were slashed with the same material. I thought the colour suited me and I was pleased with my appearance. I had not worn the gown before having kept it for a special occasion; and even now I hesitated to wear it, knowing my hostess preferred dark colours. Almost I changed it for a pale grey but decided against such an action; for once I was determined to look my best.

I was putting the finishing touches to my hair when the door opened and Prudence came in, looking faintly surprised as she saw me.

'Is that a new gown? You look really pretty, Anne.'

'Do I?' I asked, laughing. 'Yes, perhaps I do — I feel pretty tonight.'

'I wanted to give you this,' Prudence said, offering me a small parcel. 'I bought it for you in Town and kept it as a going-home-present.'

'For me? Thank you, Prudence. What is it?'

She laughed. 'Open it and see!'

I smiled and undid the wrappings carefully, giving a cry of delight as I saw the book inside. It was a copy of Richard Crawshaw's poems *Wishes for the supposed Mistress*; a book I had wished for but never read. I lifted the cover and let my eyes glide over the first line, thinking how much Jeremy would prefer the work of this Catholic poet to Milton's puritanical outpourings.

'It is just what I wanted. Thank you, Prue,' I said, kissing her. 'I shall treasure it always.'

Prudence smiled and I saw the glow of happiness in her eyes. Something was different about her this evening. She looked truly alive in a way I had not seen her since before her wedding.

'You look happy, Prue.'

'Do I?' She veiled her eyes with her

lashes. 'I'm looking forward to the party. Aren't you?'

'Yes, I am — except I do hope Lady Harrington doesn't mean to force some poor man to spend all the evening with me.'

Prudence pulled a face at me. 'She doubtless will. I warn you, Anne, she has decided it's time you were wed. I believe that's why she wanted to give this party. She likes you. I heard her telling Philip what an admirable girl you were. I expect she wishes he'd married you instead of me.'

'Prudence!' I cried. 'You shouldn't say such things even in fun.'

'Well, it's true. I know she likes you more than me — but I don't mind. You said you wanted to marry one day, Anne. I'm sure my dear mother-in-law would be delighted to arrange a match for you. Haven't you heard all those sly hints of hers?'

I laughed and turned away to pick up my fan. I had heard them, of course, but I ignored her pointed remarks if

I could. I sometimes felt it unlikely I would wed. Unless Jeremy came back to claim me as his wife I had determined to remain unwed, for I believed in my heart that I could never love another man as I loved my Cavalier, and after what had happened between us I considered myself his wife in thought and deed if not in name. And though there were times when I despaired of ever seeing him again, so long was it since that night we had parted in pain, I would not let myself admit the possibility of his death. His memory was enshrined in my heart, made even more glorious perhaps because our time together had been so brief.

But as I followed Prudence from the room my thoughts tonight were not with Jeremy. It was many years since I had attended a party such as the one the Harringtons gave this evening, and I was excited as I took my sister's arm and descended to the hall with her. Prudence was as excited as I, her pretty face flushed with colour and her eyes glowing with an inner joy.

'I shall miss you when I go, Prue,' I said.

'But you'll come again soon, dearest Anne,' she replied, giving my arm a squeeze; but somehow I knew her mind was not with me.

However, I had no time to ponder her strangely preoccupied manner, for we had reached the great chamber where the Harrington's guests were gathered. The long, elegant room was lit by many candles; the flames flickering on portraits, heavy drapes, flashing jewels, costly gowns, many of them not in the sombre hues I had expected, and the faces of so many people that I was suddenly shy. The noise of their talk and laughter swelled out to reach us even before we entered the room, drawing us on.

Lady Harrington herself was tonight wearing a splendid gown of dark blue velvet, and round her throat was wound a long string of creamy pearls. I was not really surprised to see her in colours, for though I knew her to be of the Puritan faith, she had told me she did not consider it necessary always to wear black or grey, though she invariably did so when she attended church. She tried to insist on Prudence doing likewise, but with little success. Philip was too indulgent a husband to force my sister to obey his mother's wishes in such a matter.

During my visit I had warmed towards Philip, despite his rather pompous manner, for I saw that he worshipped Prudence and was truly good to her. Lady Harrington's manner could indeed be chilling, but for myself I had no reason to complain since she seemed to like me. Therefore, I had no qualms as I saw her bearing down on me, though Prudence took the chance to escape as she came up to us.

'Ah, Anne my dear, I have found you at last,' Lady Harrington said, an arch smile curving her lips. 'Come with me — there's someone I want you to meet.'

I smiled, following my hostess dutifully through the throng of guests. She stopped a few times to exchange words with those who pressed her, forced to introduce me and spend some time in talk; but I could tell she was impatient at these delays and I guessed I was about to be presented to a young man Lady Harrington believed a suitable match for me. Having been forewarned by Prudence I did not really mind, for I knew my hostess's intentions were worthy, if misplaced. And as I should shortly be returning to my home, I didn't feel myself in any danger of being obliged to received the attentions of Lady Harrington's choice. Once I was at Withington, Philip's mother would cease to concern herself with my marriage.

Lady Harrington was detained yet again and as I glanced across the room I chanced to see my sister in conversation with a man some years her senior. He was tall, strikingly handsome and richly dressed in black velvet; but the sombre hue of his clothes was belied by the exquisite lace he wore at wrists and throat, and by the mocking sparkle in his blue eyes. Even from a distance I felt the pull of his personality, and I could see by Prudence's smile that she was enchanted with her companion. Watching her, as I was, Philip's brow was creased with a frown, and I thought that my sister was unwise to show her pleasure so plainly. Surely she must be aware of Philip's jealousy!

'It's high time the war was done with. What say you, Mistress Taverne?'

I became aware of the plump and jocular figure at my side, recognising him as Mr Harold Pettigrew, a neighbour of Sir Robert's who had taken no part in the war.

'Oh — yes, sir,' I replied, blushing as he gave my arm a squeeze. 'There can be little point in dragging out this terrible war any longer.'

'Quite right, quite right,' Mr Pettigrew

agreed. 'As I was saying to Sir Robert only yesterday 'tis time His Majesty was restored to the throne and an agreement reached with Parliament. We should heal the rift.'

I was subjected to a short homily on the rights and wrongs of both sides, to which I listened patiently. Accustomed to my grandfather's rigid ideals and having been subjected to too many of Croxley's harsh sermons, I found Mr Pettigrew a reasonable and sensible man who wanted only justice and freedom for all Englishmen. He seemed to me to be well informed and I was surprised to learn that a document aimed at bringing peace with justice and a return to all that was good in the old ways had been drawn up and offered to the King for his approval.

'And will he sign it, sir?' I asked, intrigued to learn more.

'If he truly desires what is best for England . . . ' Mr Pettigrew broke off in mid-sentence as my hostess fixed him with one of her stares. 'But I am boring you, Mistress Taverne. I must delay you no longer.'

I had not been bored but I could see that Lady Harrington was waiting, and so I smiled at my companion and allowed her to hurry me on, my curiosity beginning to be aroused. Who was this mysterious person she was so anxious for me to meet? I glanced towards the fireplace where I had last seen Prudence, finding that she had disappeared, and that her companion was nowhere to be seen. Puzzled, I was not immediately aware that Lady Harrington had stopped walking, and I bumped into someone, putting out my hands to steady myself.

'Pray forgive me — I wasn't looking where I was going!' I cried, looking up hurriedly, my cheeks aflame as I realised I had trodden on a man's shoe. 'Oh . . .'

If I had been embarrassed by my clumsiness it was nothing to the emotions which shocked me rigid as I stared into the face of my victim.

It seemed that this man and I were fated to meet in less than pleasant circumstances.

'Anne, this is the gentleman I wanted you to meet,' Lady Harrington said, smiling at me. 'His name is Colonel Lawrence and he is a distant cousin of mine. We have at long last persuaded him to spare the time to visit us . . . ' She broke off, becoming aware of my white face and the crackling tension between us.

'Good-evening, Mistress Taverne,' Christian said, recovering himself whilst I was still trying to control my shaking hands. ''Tis a pleasure to meet with you once more. I hope you are well?'

Lady Harrington looked at me and then at Christian, a frown of surprise on her high brow. 'You mean — you already know each other?'

In other circumstances I could have laughed at the chagrin in her voice and her look of disappointment, but at this moment I could not even smile.

'We have met before,' Christian said,

and I heard the wry note in his voice as he saw my frozen lips.

I tried to answer or to smile for politeness' sake, but I was bereft of words. The shock of coming upon him so unexpectedly had made me feel odd. For one terrible moment as his face misted to a blur and the room span round crazily I thought I was about to faint. I heard Lady Harrington's voice as from a great distance.

'I don't understand. I meant to suggest you should escort Mistress Taverne into supper, Colonel Lawrence.'

'An excellent idea, Lady Harrington,' Christian replied easily, and I envied him his command of the emotions which I saw working in his eyes. 'Mistress Taverne, you will give me the honour I trust?'

I stared up at him almost stupidly, the colour coming back to my cheeks in a great rush which made me feel hot with embarrassment. Then I saw the challenging look in his eyes and pride gave me the courage to fight my craven urge to turn and run. I forced stiff lips to a smile, murmuring my assent as I laid the tips of my fingers on his arm, feeling the softness of velvet. I had no choice but to go with him: to refuse would be needlessly rude to both him and my hostess.

As we moved away through the crowded room, he glanced down at me, his face grave. 'I am indebted to you for your forbearance, Mistress Taverne — but I do realise this meeting must be distasteful to you. Believe me, had I but known you were here I would not have come tonight.'

I stood still for a moment, gazing up at him thoughtfully. 'The war is over, Colonel Lawrence.'

He studied my face, frowning. 'Then — what are you saying? Are we no longer enemies? You do not hate me?'

'I believe I never hated you, sir,' I said, realising it was true. 'If I was harsh to you it was my grief which spoke. I was angry and in pain. Anger fades in time — but sorrow remains.'

'Ah yes, grief remains. Sometimes it leaves you for a space and you think it gone — then memory stirs and the pain returns, sharpened by absence.'

Gazing up into his eyes which were just now the colour of a wintry sky, I saw pain there, and I recoiled as I felt it touch me for a moment. I felt I was seeing the inner man naked of all pretence and I did not want to see so deeply into this man's soul: it disturbed me too much. Somehow I knew he had suffered in a manner beyond my comprehension, and something within me reached out to him in compassion despite myself. He smiled as if he too felt the brief meeting of our souls and was refreshed by it.

'Thank you,' he said.

'For what pray?' I was reluctant to admit that I had known a moment of perfect communion with him.

He saw my reluctance and smiled oddly. 'You've stopped being angry with me.'

His simple words brought the truth

home to me more completely than an hour of searching my conscience might have done. I laughed, realising that I was glad to be at ease with him.

'Yes, I believe I have.'

For a moment our eyes met and held again, then I turned away. I was no longer angry with him, but I had remembered the causes for my anger. We had drawn close for a small space of time, but friendship between us was not possible: my father's death, Sir John's anger and the bitterness of war lay between us.

By now we had reached the dining-chamber; a long room with pine panelling and carved pilasters ornamented with swags of flowers and acanthus leaves. In the centre of the room two heavy tables with bulbous supports had been pushed together to accommodate all the guests. At each end of the table were the chairs normally used by Sir Robert and his wife, but tonight given up to the most important guests after the custom of the time.

We made our way further down the table, sitting on the wooden stools provided for general use, all chance of private conversation ended now that we had close companions on either side with whom we must converse.

The meal seemed to me to drag on endlessly as platter after platter of rich food was brought to table; roast meats, pastries, soups, pigeons swimming in a wine sauce. A profusion of dishes both sweet and savoury to delight the palate of a gourmet, washed down by a fine French wine which must have cost Sir Robert a fortune in such times as these. I picked at what was set before me, my gaze wandering down the candlelit table over faces and shadows, the gush of merry chatter washing about me as the waves of the sea, unheard and distant. I smiled and answered when a question was addressed to me, hardly knowing whether my reply made sense to my questioner. I was aware only of the man sitting beside me, silent also as if in answer to my mood.

I saw Prudence, her smile dimmed as she sat at her husband's side, her mouth turned down sulkily as I had often seen it; but I looked in vain for the man I had noticed her with earlier. He seemed not to have stayed to sup with us and I wondered why, intending to ask Prudence about him privately before I left.

'Mistress Taverne?'

I turned my head as I became aware of Sir Robert's servant at my side. He held out a letter to me as I inclined my head in assent. 'Yes, I am Anne Taverne.'

'Forgive my intrusion at table, mistress,' he said, looking awkward. 'The messenger who brought this letter said it was most urgent!'

I stared at him in surprise, my heart jerking wildly as I saw the seal of Sir John's crest. This letter had come from Withington!

'Thank you. I will read it now . . . ' I forced myself to smile at the servant as he hovered nervously at my side, perhaps awaiting further instructions.

I broke open the wax seal, scanning the contents with feverish haste, already afraid of what they contained. Mercy had written to me from Withington begging me to return home as swiftly as I might, and I knew what such a message must mean even before I reached the end. Giving a cry of alarm, I got to my feet, the letter fluttering from my nerveless fingers as I ran from the room.

Fortunately Lady Harrington saw me leave and followed me at once, concern on her face as she caught me at the foot of the stairs.

'What ails you, my dear?' she asked. 'You are not ill?'

'No indeed, madam.' In my sudden panic I had forgotten my manners. 'Forgive me for leaving the table so rudely — I've received an urgent summons from home. Sir John has been taken ill again. I must go to him at once.'

'So that was it — the letter.' Lady

Harrington frowned, and I knew she was annoyed that the letter had been brought straight to me without her consent. 'I know how anxious you must be, Anne, but you will not think of leaving us tonight — in the morning will be time enough. After all, what can you hope to do — only God's will can decide whether it is time for your grandfather to die.'

'I must go to him tonight!' My voice was unusually sharp. I knew she hadn't meant to sound so unfeeling but I was racked with guilt that Sir John was lying ill while I pleasured myself at the Harrington's party. I wanted to be with my grandfather even if I could do no more than hold his hand.

'But the journey will be hazardous and you must go alone for neither Sir Robert nor I can leave our guests.'

'Perhaps you would allow me to escort you, Mistress Taverne.'

Christian's quiet voice stopped Lady Harrington's complaint. He was standing a little behind us, watching gravely.

Lady Harrington turned to look at him, relief on her face as she saw the way out of her dilemma. In all conscience she could not let me go alone but with her kinsman's escort the matter was solved to her liking.

'Would you be so kind, Colonel?' She smiled at him. 'It would ease my mind immeasurably to know Mistress Taverne was under your protection.'

'If Mistress Taverne is willing?'

'Well, my dear?' Lady Harrington looked up at me.

I saw that I had no choice. I had travelled here with Greta and the protection of one of Sir Robert's friends. I should not be allowed to leave unless I accepted Christian's offer. Philip was to have seen me home tomorrow himself, but I could not demand that he leave his home in the middle of a reception. I must give in with what grace I could muster.

'Thank you, Colonel Lawrence,' I said. 'If you will be so good as to wait while I fetch my cloak and tell my maid to make ready, I shall be glad of your services.'

'Do not bother your head about your clothes; I will have them sent on,' Lady Harrington said, happy now that I was to do her bidding. 'Take only what is necessary for your immediate comfort, my dear. I shall have the carriage ordered at once — and send your sister to you. Mrs Harrington will no doubt want a few moments alone with you before you leave. You will not expect her to accompany you I trust.'

It was hardly a question, both of us knew Prudence could not stand the strain of a long journey under such uncomfortable circumstances. 'No. I should be glad of an opportunity to speak with her, but it will be best if she remains here. I will send news if . . . ' I could not go on and Lady Harrington pressed my hands with a show of feeling.

'If necessary I shall bring Prudence to Withington myself — but I agree that it is better for her to stay here just now.'

I hesitated, not liking the cold note which had entered her voice, nor the hard set of her mouth. 'Please do not be too harsh with her, Lady Harrington,' I said slowly, a little sorry that I must leave my sister behind. 'She has always been a — a little petulant, but she is a good girl at heart.'

'Of course.' Lady Harrington's face closed and she was the polite hostess saying farewell to her guest. 'But do not let us delay you further, Anne.'

I nodded. Prudence belonged here now and I could do nothing to smooth her path, only patience and understanding would heal the breach between these two, and I doubted they were qualities shared by either lady.

Looking at Christian, I smiled slightly. 'Excuse me, sir. I shall not keep you waiting long.'

He inclined his head, his face still grave. 'I am at your disposal, Mistress Taverne.'

I hesitated a moment more, wondering at the perversity of Fate; then I turned and fled up the stairs, all thoughts of Christian Lawrence banished from mind by the anxiety I felt for Sir John.

* * *

Prudence wept in my arms before I left Brooklands, but I was not sure whether she cried for Grandfather, me, or herself. The happiness I had seen in her earlier had gone, to be replaced by a sullen quietness. I would have questioned her further, but there was little time and my mind was at Withington. So with tears, hugs and kisses, I tore myself from my sister's arms and went out to the courtyard where the carriage was waiting.

Christian Lawrence stood talking to the coachman; giving him last minute instructions I doubted not. He came towards Greta and myself, helping first me and then my little, kitchen maid into the carriage. Greta was overcome by his courtesy to her, more than she'd received from the gentleman who had escorted us here, shrinking into her corner of the carriage as if she was made shy by the presence of the Colonel, who had decided to ride inside with us for at least this first stage of our journey.

★ ★ ★

Sir Robert and Lady Harrington had both made their good-byes to me inside, and I'd left a tearful Prudence in my chamber so there was no one but a servant to wave us farewell. I settled back against the squabs, preparing for the long and tedious journey which lay ahead. It would hold a nightmarish quality for me, I knew, since I was possessed by a terrible fear that I would arrive too late. My one fear was that Sir John would die without me at his side.

Luckily for us the moon was full

and round, giving a pale silver light on grass, trees, hedges and rooftops alike. The horses would not miss their footing or overturn the carriage in a deep rut; but the coachman had obviously been told to drive at a steady pace, which seemed painfully slow to me in my impatience to be at Withington. Yet I knew that even if we drove all night and stopped only briefly to change the horses we could not reach our destination before tomorrow night.

'I should never have left him alone,' I said, hardly realising that I'd spoken aloud. 'Prudence didn't really need me.'

Christian could not be expected to understand my ambiguous speech, but he sensed the guilt behind it. 'You could not know Sir John would become ill while you were away,' he said quietly, looking at me from the opposite seat. 'And even if you had been with him there is no guarantee that your presence would have made the slightest difference.'

'No,' I whispered. Lady Harrington had said something similar to me, but somehow I did not resent it as much from my grave companion. 'Ne'er a blanket wash in May, lest the head of the house you wash away.'

'I beg your pardon?' Christian stared at me, bewildered.

I gave a strangled laugh which might have been a sob. 'It was something Bessie said — she is my maid, housekeeper, friend and conscience all in one — when I fetched the blankets down to the wash tub before I came away. She begged me to think twice about such foolishness, but I wouldn't listen. I laughed at her. It was such a lovely day and they all dried before dusk.' I drew in my breath sharply. 'I should not have laughed 'twas tempting the Devil.'

'These tales are superstition — nothing more. You have nothing to blame yourself for.'

I fiddled with my gloves, tearing at the fringed tassels destructively. 'Bessie

265

is very superstitious. She won't let me bring hawthorn blossom into the house because it's unlucky. Silly isn't it?'

'Village folk thrive on such nonsense,' Christian said, ignoring the little gasp from Greta in her corner. 'When I was a babe my nurse used to hang yarrow over my cradle to protect me from evil spirits — and she told me that if ever I was cursed by a witch the surest way to break the spell was to carry a bag of rosemary and marigold petals inside my shirt. Oh, and to add a few drops of human blood to my ale!'

I smiled, knowing he was talking just for the sake of it, trying to lift my spirits. I decided to go along with him, anything rather than let my thoughts dwell where they could do little good. 'I never heard of that before; though Bessie says that picking scabious invites a visit from the Devil, and whenever Prudence or I went near the river when we were small she used to warn us that a monster called *Jenny Greenteeth* would get us.'

Christian laughed outright and oddly I was comforted by the sound, and by his presence in the carriage. 'Today she would probably have warned you about Old Noll. I've heard country folk talk of his eating babes for his supper when they want to frighten children into obedience.'

I glanced at him curiously. 'You don't mind that?'

'No.' Christian smiled at me. 'Oliver is my friend — but at times he even frightens me.'

'Why?' My curiosity was aroused now.

'He is a man of high ideals; I find it difficult to live up to them.'

I digested this in silence. For myself I believed him a man with strong principles, though I knew from harsh experience that he made his own rules. I lifted my head and looked straight at him. 'I thought all Puritans believed themselves the chosen ones of God?'

My challenge was a provocative one, for the attitude of Croxley and his ilk annoyed me.

'I am not a Puritan. I fought on Parliament's side because I stand for the right of all Englishmen to have a free parliament, just laws and the right of choice in matters of religion.'

I was surprised, though I had no right to be. Why should I have thought him a Puritan? Perhaps it was because I had first seen him in the buff coat and pot helmet worn by Cromwell's men, and I had been taught to distrust all who wore the trappings of Parliament. Even Mr Pettigrew, who had seemed such a reasonable man to me, was a Puritan; though not as fanatical as our parson at Withington.

'I have heard that Cromwell himself would like to see His Majesty restored to the throne if he will but come to terms. Is that true?'

'I believe he has some such hope. Unfortunately, the King is a stubborn man.'

'So you think the talks will come to nothing. What then — another war?'

'Perhaps.' Christian frowned. 'I hope not.'

I made no reply. The prospect of another war breaking out was so terrible to me that I could not believe it would happen. Surely saner counsels must prevail — there had been enough bloodshed!

'I have not offended you by speaking plainly?'

I blinked at him, tears hovering on my lashes. 'No — I was thinking of war and my father — and Sir John. If he should die . . . '

'Try not to worry too much. We have many hours of travelling before us: you should get what rest you can.'

I pulled back the blue velvet curtains to peer out of the coach windows. The flat fields were beginning to give way to gentle wooded slopes. Despite the lateness of the hour the sky was bright, almost white and cloudless. The air had a hint of rain in it and I prayed it would hold off for as long as possible. Rain could only hinder us and delay our journey. I let the curtain go and sat back with a sigh.

'I should never have left him,' I said uselessly.

Christian was silent. Perhaps he realised that words were of little help to me now.

The carriage rumbled on through the night, occasionally lurching over a rut in the road and pitching us forward. Inside the silence deepened and lengthened. Greta was snoring gently in her corner. I closed my eyes and tried to sleep.

★ ★ ★

It was daylight when I wakened, a gentle hand shaking me to awareness as the coach slowed to a jolting halt. I saw that Christian was now sitting by my side, and I had hazy recollections of my head resting on his shoulder as I slept.

'We have stopped to change the horses,' he said, a slight smile playing about his mouth as he saw my quick flush. 'We shall get out and refresh ourselves while we wait.'

I opened my mouth to protest, then decided against it. A short break would make little difference to our journey and my body was aching all over from the jolting of the coach.

'Yes — it will be better for us all,' I agreed.

Christian helped me out, turning back to assist Greta once I was safely on my feet. He stayed only to give the coachman brief instructions before leading us both into the inn. The landlord came bustling to greet us, eager to serve customers rich enough to travel in their own coach. Arrangements were made for the change of horses, and for a meal for us. Then the lady of the house came to take me upstairs to a private chamber where I could wash my hands and face and make what repairs I needed for my comfort.

Soon I was back in the inn parlour, eating my cold bacon and coddled eggs with some fresh baked bread and a tankard of ale. Since I had eaten little the previous evening I found this plain fare much to my taste and ate readily, as did both Greta and Christian. We spoke very seldom, for there was nothing to be said. Polite conversation would have seemed out of place in the quietness of the parlour, and I had no wish for it.

When Greta and I went back to the carriage, Christian mounted a chestnut gelding he had hired from the landlord. He rode beside the carriage all day, and I guessed he was on the watch for any sign of trouble, though he made no mention of it to me; but I knew that the war had left many potentially dangerous men in its wake. Beggars, wounded soldiers who would never again find work, men who had lost everything they had because of the struggle betwixt King and Parliament; any of them might seek recompense for their misfortune from an unwary traveller.

We stopped once more to change our horses, but this time I did not get out. Refreshments were brought to the window, but I wanted nothing. Once more I was in a fever of impatience to be at home. Darkness fell and Christian rode with me again, his horse trotting behind the carriage. I slept once and woke to find his arm around me. I moved away from him, but said nothing.

The first rays of the sun were streaking the sky with a rosy glow when the carriage slowed to a halt for the last time. Christian opened the carriage door and got out, helping me down.

'Sir John is a strong man,' he said as he saw my look of apprehension. 'He may well have recovered.'

'Thank you for your kindness . . . ' I began, but even as I did so the front door opened and I saw Mercy waiting for me. 'Excuse me . . . '

I ran from him to Mercy's arms. She embraced me, drawing me into the house as she untied the strings of my cloak and gently took it from me.

'Grandfather?' I asked fearfully.

'A little better since I wrote to you I think — but he's still very ill, Anne. I thought it my duty to send for you, though I was loth to upset you.'

'You did as you thought best and I am grateful,' I said, smiling a little as Mercy fussed round me. 'Was it another seizure?'

'No. Babbage says 'tis an inflamation of the lungs — but I'm not sure which is worse. I've feared for him, Anne.'

'I must go to him.' I glanced over my shoulder at the man standing awkwardly just inside the hall door. 'Please forgive me, Colonel. Mercy will make you comfortable. I shall see you later.'

'Pray do not be concerned for me,

Mistress Taverne.'

I gave him a fleeting smile, going quickly from the room, little dreaming that when I came back down to the parlour he would be gone.

7

PERHAPS I should not have been surprised that Christian had gone by the time I came down from my grandfather's room. He had done what he could for me, wanting no thanks, and knowing, as I had, that friendship between us was impossible. If he had stayed I must have offered him the hospitality of Sir John's house, and that while Grandfather lay close to death. His own sense of decency had prevented him from accepting such hospitality or compelling me to offer it.

While I sat by Sir John's bedside, watching his laboured breathing, I had no thought for the man who had escorted me home. Mercy had been right to send for me, I knew this as soon as I entered Grandfather's room. Hoddle had done all he could to make his master comfortable; but I saw the welcoming light in Sir John's eyes, though he was too ill to speak more than my name, and I knew he was glad to have me there. Perhaps there was little practical help I could give, but I was there and I knew how much it meant to him.

I sat beside him until he slept, holding the frail hand in mine and saying little. He smiled at me, his dark-veined lids fluttering against pale cheeks; then he passed into a peaceful sleep, the first for some days, as Mercy told me later.

'You look tired to death,' she cried when I went down to the parlour. 'You must get some rest, Anne. I'll call you if you're needed.'

'I am very tired,' I agreed with a sigh. 'I will rest in a moment — but first I must thank Colonel Lawrence properly. I was too distraught to think clearly when we arrived. Where is he? You have made him comfortable?'

Mercy looked unhappy, and then she

told me he had gone. 'I asked him to stay awhile and rest, but he would go straight way.'

I frowned. 'Did he leave no message for me?'

'I asked him what I should say to you and he said, 'Say only that I wish her well, madam.' Then he went out before I could think of a reply. My wits must have been awandering to let him go, the poor man. Forgive me, Anne.'

I shook my head, my surprise fading as I thought of what was in his mind and knew that he had acted wisely. Lady Harrington had forced us to accept a situation which was uncomfortable for us both. I very much doubted that I should ever see Colonel Lawrence again and I found that I was sorry. If things had been otherwise I could have valued him as my friend. I liked his grave manner and the way his grey eyes could suddenly light with laughter.

Bessie brought me a little cold

chicken and a glass of wine. She scolded me for the dark rings beneath my eyes, but I could see that she too was pleased to have me home. I ate my meal and drank the wine, feeling its warmth spread through my weary body; then I went up to my own room to rest. I thought of Christian Lawrence for a time before I closed my eyes, but his face faded from my mind as sleep overcame me and in the following days and weeks I was to have scant leisure to think of him again.

For many days and weary nights I was afraid to leave the house lest my grandfather should weaken and let slip his fragile hold on life whilst I was gone. His racking cough was painful to hear, and the vile yellow phlegm he spat into my bowl was sometimes tinged with blood. I used all my skills with herbs to nurse him through the fever, and found them little enough. Grandfather swallowed all the mixtures I gave him, complaining not at all, and it was his very docility which alarmed me more than all the rest. I was afraid that he was tired of living, that he would surrender to the inevitable and give up the fight for life; but I had forgotten his stubbornness, and once the fever had broken so the will to recover grew strong in him again.

Through all this time Mercy and Doctor Babbage came regularly to the house to give what comfort and cheer they could, both to grandfather and myself. I was grateful for their support, and I did not know what I should have done without them. Nat and his wife came too, bringing their good wishes and some wild fowl Nat had snared. Sir Mathew Attwood, an old friend of my grandfather's, travelled over twenty miles to visit with him for a short while. During the war we had seen little of Sir Mathew since he had sided with Parliament, but now he came to talk and gossip and offer me his help if I should ever need it. I thanked him for his kindness, but I knew that I would never avail myself of his offer. I was not alone in the world and should not be if Sir John died. I had good friends and my aunt, who would like nothing better than to have me stay beneath her roof. I had written to Aunt Sophia to tell her of Grandfather's illness, and though she had not yet replied, I knew exactly what she would say.

Of course Parson Croxley came most dutifully to pay his respects at least three times each week, though I would not allow him to see Sir John until he was beginning to recover, preferring to endure the tedium of these visits myself rather than inflict them on Grandfather. But perhaps I was ungrateful and let my dislike of our parson cloud my judgement. Sometimes his sister came with him; a pale, thin shadow beside her brother, echoing his sentiments with more duty than real sincerity. I tried to be friends with her, but she neatly fended all my attempts to reach her, settling her hands primly in the folds of her stiff black silk gown and closing her lips together in a narrow line.

And so the days passed and Grandfather was a little better, sitting up against the pillows now to take the nourishing broth Bessie made especially for him. I read him the letters I had received from Lady Harrington and Prudence, inquiring after his health, and I talked to him of my visit there, reading a few lines from the poem my sister had given me.

'Who'er she be,
That not impossible She
That shall command my heart and
  me;

Where'er she lie,
Locked up from mortal eye
In shady leaves of destiny:

Till that ripe birth
Of studied fate stand forth,
And teach her fair steps tread our
  earth;

Till that divine
Idea take shrine
Of crystal flesh, through which to
  shine.'

Sir John took my hand in his gently.
''Tis time you were wed, Anne. I've
been selfish holding you here with me
— a selfish old man. You've had
no life.'

'Hush, Grandfather.' My hand
tightened on his and I smiled at him.
'I'm happy here with you. I don't want
to be wed just yet.'

'When I'm better you must go to
your aunt,' he said. 'She'll find you
a good husband. Yes, that's what you
must do, Anne.'

'We'll see,' I promised to quiet
him, knowing I would always win
this particular argument. 'It's time
for your rest now, dearest. I'm going
for a little walk.'

'Yes, a walk will do you good.' He
sighed and settled back against the
pillows. 'Come up to me again later,

Anne, and read me some more of your poem — it hath a pleasant ring to it.'

'Of course.' I bent to kiss his cheek, passing Hoddle as I left the room. 'He'll sleep now I think.'

Hoddle inclined his head, 'I'll be here if he needs me.'

'I know.'

I went out and closed the door gently, aware of the faint note of reproach in his voice. Hoddle could never quite accept my presence in Sir John's chamber.

I went to my own chamber, splashing my face and hands with cool water and tidying my hair before collecting my shawl. I glanced at myself in the hand mirror, noting the neat appearance of my simple blue gown and white lace bertha, my thick mane of dark hair tucked beneath a cap of the same lace, and I sighed. I was two and twenty, well past the age for marrying; soon I should have settled into the life of a maiden aunt; a companion to my grandfather, on hand as a nurse and comforter to my sister's children. Even Prudence had taken it for granted I did not intend to wed. Grandfather had realised my need for a husband and children of my own, but I knew he would soon forget if I left the subject alone. No matter how lonely I sometimes was I could not think of taking a husband. How could I when my heart was given to Jeremy?

I pushed the thought from my mind, I had examined it so often in the close-curtained privacy of my bed. In almost two years I'd had no word from Jeremy. Was I a fool to keep his memory sacred in my heart? Although I had lived quietly at home with Grandfather, I had not entirely been shut off from the world. There were at least three widowers with small children in the district who called on us from time to time; I knew that with a little encouragement I might have had an offer of marriage from any one of them these past eighteen months. And Sir Mathew Attwood's visit had not been one merely of sympathy: he had a nephew of three and twenty, a young man of more personality than fortune who had called on me twice in the last six months. As Sir John's likely heir, Withington not being entailed to the nearest male relative, I would make a suitable wife for Henry Attwood.

Suddenly I laughed. What a fool I was to let an idle remark of Prudence's cloud my judgement. At two and twenty I was young enough to take my time in the weighty matter of choosing a husband. Time enough to decide when Grandfather was well again.

I went down to the kitchen, smiling at my own fancies. What need had I of a husband? I was happy as mistress of Withington, and I was looking forward to my walk this afternoon. During Sir John's illness I had exhausted my supply of marjoram, a useful painkiller, and agrimony, which I brewed in to a fragrant herb tea. Neither of these plants grew in my garden and now that I felt I could safely leave the house, I intended to go in search of them along the hedgerows. It was a fine day for walking, a light breeze tempering the heat.

As I entered the kitchen Bessie slammed the back door and I heard her say sharply, 'She can't see you today. I've told you before not to come here. Be off with you!'

'Who was that, Bessie?' I asked, vaguely curious as to who had aroused her wrath.

Bessie jumped, looking guilty as she turned to face me. There was an odd, wary expression in her eyes as she said: 'I didn't hear you come in. 'Twas only an old gipsy woman selling her wares. I told her we lacked nothing but she was very persistent.'

I frowned. Somehow I was sure Bessie was lying to me. Her face was flushed and she could not look at me. But why should she lie about something so unimportant?

I decided it was my imagination. 'I thought I'd walk to Brockhill Woods,'

I said, bending to take up the rush basket I used for collecting herbs and wild plants.

'Aye, the walk will do you good,' Bessie said, a reluctant note in her voice which puzzled me. 'Will you glance at the pork jellies I made before you go? They're not setting as they ought.'

'If you wish.'

I followed Bessie into the pantry; a large, airy room with a stone floor which was always cool even on the hottest day. There on the scrubbed shelves the pots of pork jelly stood in neat rows. I looked at several, finding, as I'd half expected, that they were perfectly jellied.

'There's nothing wrong with these,' I said, looking at Bessie questioningly.

'No?' Bessie tried to sound unconcerned and failed. 'They must've set since I glanced at them earlier. This cheese is mouldy. Shall I throw it away then?'

'Yes.' I picked up my basket again,

frowning. Bessie was deliberately trying to delay me. Why? 'I'll go now — unless you need me for anything else?'

'Well, I was wondering what you'd like for your dinner, seeing as how you've eaten so little of late. There's a nice piece of salt beef or a fat capon — or mayhap you'd prefer a chicken pie or a pastie?'

'What is the matter?' I asked, sure now that my suspicions were correct. 'Why don't you want me to leave?'

'I don't know why you should think that, Mistress Anne.' Bessie assumed an air of hurt surprise. 'I was only thinking of how best to tempt your appetite. I'm sure I never meant no harm.'

I pulled a wry face at her. She was behaving very oddly, but she obviously had no intention of telling me why. 'The chicken pie sounds good, Bessie — and perhaps a soup for Sir John?'

'Aye, I'll see to that right enough. A good nourishing broth to give him strength.'

I murmured my thanks and left since Bessie made no further attempts to delay me. Greta was in the scullery, scouring pans and singing as she worked, the sunlight warm through the window on her little plain face. Her sojurn at Brooklands as my personal maid seemed to have changed her not one whit: she was happiest in her own scullery with only Bessie to scold her. I smiled as I passed and she paused in her singing to wish me good-bye.

I could still hear her song as I went out into the garden. It made me smile as I stopped to let my eyes feast on the riot of colour all around me: pinks, reds and delicate mauves as the roses competed for space with tall foxgloves and sweet-brier. I bent to inhale the scent of a perfect, dark red rose, thinking I would pick some for Sir John's room when I returned. They would bring a little beauty into his confined world.

My heart rising with the prospect of an afternoon of complete freedom before me, I let myself out of a little side gate into the close-hedged lane beyond. I had to stand to one side as a young stable lad passed me, giving me a cheery greeting as he led one of the farm horses down to the blacksmith in the village. I waved to him as he went by, turning away in the opposite direction.

Brookhill Woods lay some little distance away, and it would take me at least half an hour to reach them, but I should enjoy the walk and the fresh air. The sky above me was a hazy blue, the sun warm on my face as I strolled unhurriedly through the long grass of the meadows. Above me a lark was singing sweetly, hovering in the clear air as it gave praise for the day. I too was giving praise for the glory of such a day, my senses lulled by the peace of the countryside, a peace I hoped would never again be shattered by the horrors of civil war. Not so long ago troops of soldiers had flattened this grass which now clung about my ankles and dampened the hem of my gown; there had been a bitter battle between a small party of Royalists and one of the local trained bands. We had heard the noise of guns firing, and Nat had gone with some of the other men to investigate when night fell. He told me they had found a score of men already dead or dying, those who were still able to ride having ridden off into the night. They did what they could for the badly injured, but none had survived. I prayed that our peaceful village would never again be the scene of such carnage.

Seeing a farmer and his son at work scything the long grass in preparation for the haymaking. I paused to watch and exchange a greeting, remembering long sunny days in my childhood when I worked at my father's side to gather in the sweet-smelling hay. Since the war the meadows beyond Withington had been left to go wild: we had no men to make or gather in the hay. But soon now we should start to work the fields again. Nat said the men were returning to their homes, despite the army not yet having been disbanded. Soon we would be able to hire men from our own village again, and then life would be as it was before the war.

It was cooler in the woods, but here and there the sun filtered through the trees to make bright patches on the ground. I saw the tall spikes of Viper's Bugloss and bent to gather a few of the vivid blue flowers.

Hearing the rattling trill of a wood warbler I glanced up, catching a brief glimpse of his yellow throat and white breast before he took fright and flew away. I smiled, thinking how quiet and tranquil it was in these lovely woods. I walked on a little further, finding a patch of bright willow herb, or codlins and cream as it is sometimes called because the flowers resemble those of a red-blossomed cooking apple. Adding a few stalks of calamint to my basket, I inhaled its minty fragrance which was so refreshing when the herb was used for making tea. Then I paused to watch a butterfly sipping nectar from the feathery flowers of meadow-sweet, distinguishable only by the orange tips of its creamy wings. My basket was almost full now as bramble leaves, comfrey, balm and speedwell joined the other herbs.

Suddenly I heard the snap of a twig as though someone had trodden on a dry branch. I glanced around uneasily, feeling I was not alone, though I could see no one. There was no answer to my call of, 'Who's there?' and I glanced up at the sky, realising that the sun had moved round and was dipping in the west. Remembering the incident in the churchyard just before I went to stay with Prudence, I felt again that someone was watching me, but though I called once more I had no reply. I began to retrace my steps through the woods, my heart beating a little unsteadily as I became aware of the lateness of the hour. Engrossed in my search for herbs and wild flowers I had not noticed the time slipping by. I stopped only to gather a handful of the nettles which had proved so beneficial in the cure for inflamation of the lungs, then I left the woods and began the long walk home.

No one was in sight as I passed the hayfield. The farmer and his son had finished their work and gone for their supper, leaving the grass in neat swathes, ready to be turned. I walked quickly now, anxious because I'd stayed away longer than I'd intended.

The sky was slowly darkening and the warmth had gone from the day. Intent on reaching Withington before nightfall, I did not at first notice the shadow of a man hovering near my gate. It was only when the shadow detached itself from the sheltering trees and came towards me that I saw him. Even then I took little notice at first, thinking it only my groom or a passing villager. Then I noticed the military bearing of this shadow which was fast becoming substance as we drew nearer together, and the graceful movement of his elegant figure. I gasped as the suspicion entered my mind, and then he was so close that I could see his face. Suddenly I dropped my basket and ran towards him as he opened his arms, sweeping me against him in a fierce embrace which almost squeezed the breath from me. Then I was laughing and crying at once, tears cascading down my cheeks as I lifted my face to him, hardly believing that I was really seeing him and that it was not a dream.

'Jeremy . . . you've come back to me . . .'

He looked into my face long and hungrily, as if searching for something, the answer to a question he could not ask in words. Then his head came down and our lips met in an achingly-sweet kiss which set my senses swimming and made me weep even harder.

'My darling girl — have you missed me?' The teasing note in his voice brought my head up, eyes glistening.

'Oh, Jeremy — so much!' I choked, struggling to control my tears. 'I thought you dead . . . you sent no message.'

He stroked my hair, holding me gently to him, his lips brushing against my brow. 'It was not possible, my love. When the King was made a prisoner of the Scots I went to Jersey and thence to France. I have but recently returned to this country.' I looked up at him with a protest on my lips. Surely he could have sent some word! Others had managed it somehow. But if he saw reproach in my eyes he was determined not to acknowledge it. He drew me close to him once more, kissing me with a hungry passion which set my pulses racing and drove all thought of censure from my mind. 'I have much to tell you, my beautiful Anne, but may we not talk later? I am weary with travelling and I've not slept in a bed since I left France some six days since.'

In my joy at seeing him I had

not noticed the signs of strain in his face. Now I let my eyes travel over him, aware of the shadows beneath his eyes and his stained clothing. Love welled up in me. This was the man I had nursed through his illness, the man I had grown to love before he became restless and eager to leave me for the King's service. He needed me and because of it any doubts or anger I might have felt at his neglect of me these past two years simply melted away.

I smiled at him, then bent to retrieve my basket. 'Forgive me, Jeremy, how thoughtless I am. You must be tired and hungry.'

'And dirty,' he added with a rueful grin. 'Do you think Sir John will lend me his shirt again?'

My smile faded at the mention of Sir John. 'He has been very ill,' I said. 'But come in. There's no need for secrecy this time.'

Jeremy laid a warning hand on my arm. 'There is much need, Anne: you must tell no one that I have lately come from France.'

I gazed up at him, a little puzzled. 'Surely you know I would never betray you?'

'Yes.' He took my hand and kissed it. 'But I say this as much for your own sake as mine. I had to see you, Anne, or I would not have come. I should not have come.'

I was puzzled by something in his manner, a reserve I had never seen in him before. 'You mean there may be danger for us if it were known you had been here? Are you a spy?'

His lazy grin chased my unease away. 'No, merely a carrier of messages; but we will talk later. It is not safe to linger here: I may have been followed, though I believe all safe.'

'Then come inside, my love. You must rest and eat before you tell me your news.'

I took his hand and led him through the garden. The scent of the roses was heavy on the evening air and tiny flies beat against the lighted windows of the kitchen. I heard a rumble as if of thunder and I wondered if there would be a storm. I remembered there had been a storm the night Jeremy first came into my life. How strange if there should be another storm tonight. Polly, my groom's wife, was just leaving the house to go to her own small cottage. She looked surprised as she saw us and I told her Jeremy was a distant cousin of my mother's come on a visit. She accepted my statement without suspicion, curtseying to him and wishing him a pleasant stay; then she asked if she should prepare a bed-chamber for him and I agreed, smiling as she hurried away so as to be the first with the exciting news. We had few enough visitors at Withington to make it an occasion.

I took Jeremy in through the side door, leaving him in the parlour with a flask of wine whilst I went to warn Bessie of his arrival. She was alone when I found her and she greeted the news with frowning disapproval but no surprise: Polly had forestalled me. Greta came in then and so she was prevented from speaking too plainly, but one sniff was enough to tell me what she thought.

'Supper will be ready in half an hour,' she grunted. 'You're late back, Mistress Anne.'

Her tone conveyed much she could not put into words. 'Can you not delay the meal for a while?' I asked, giving her an appealing smile. 'Mr Allenby needs time to wash and change his clothes.'

'Mr Allenby is it?' Bessie looked put out. 'I suppose I might — if you wish it.'

'I do wish it — please.' Bessie sniffed but I saw acquiescence in her eyes. 'Perhaps Greta could be spared to carry a pitcher of warm water up to our guest's room?'

'Aye.' She sliced savagely into a freshly baked loaf. 'I'll see to it.'

I sighed and went out into the

hall, unsurprised at Bessie's reactions. For reasons of her own Bessie had taken a dislike to Jeremy almost from the start, though she'd never actually voiced her doubts to me. She had not needed to, her manner made her feelings only too plain. However, I was at this moment far too happy to let my maid's disapproval bother me. I returned to the parlour as swiftly as maybe, my heart racing as I saw the welcome in my lover's eyes. How many lonely nights had I spent praying for his return? Now he was here and my pulses were skipping like newborn lambs in spring every time he looked at me. I could not hope to hide my feelings, nor did I try. I went to him at once to take the hand he offered to me. He drew me into his arms, kissing me several times before either of us could recover our wits. At last I put him from me with shaking hands and a smile of love.

'Bessie is delaying supper, my love; but we mustn't try her patience too hard.'

Jeremy smiled at me, whisking the lace cap from my head to watch the dark locks tumble about my shoulders. 'I'm hungry for you, Anne,' he whispered.

'Later . . . ' I avoided him with a laugh. 'We shall have time enough later, Jeremy. First you must refresh yourself.'

Reluctantly, he let me go, following me from the room and up to the chamber Polly had hastily prepared for him. She was tidying the coverlet as he opened the door, and she bobbed a curtsey, her cheeks flushed as he came in with me.

'I will return later to pass a warming pan through the sheets, sir,' she said, not looking at Jeremy. 'There is hot water ready and fresh linen. Is there anything else you require?'

'No, I thank you, mistress.' He smiled at her as she passed out of the room. Then turning to me, he kissed my hand once more before he let me leave him.

When the door of his chamber had closed behind Jeremy, I went to Sir John's bedchamber. Hoddle met me at the door, a warning finger to his lips.

'The master is sleeping,' he whispered. 'He took a little broth for his supper but half an hour ago.'

'I was late returning — I didn't realise the time.'

Hoddle's mouth pursed. 'Sir John is quite comfortable, Mistress Anne. There's no need for you to concern yourself tonight.'

I thanked him, feeling relieved but knowing his look of disapproval was a rebuke. There was indeed a small seed of guilt in my mind as I went to my own room: I had promised my grandfather I would see him before supper; but at this moment I was too happy to let such a small thing upset me. Grandfather would understand when I explained how the time had slipped away.

★ ★ ★

The candles were flickering low in their sconces as I looked across the table, now scattered with the remains of our meal. I poured more wine into Jeremy's cup as he lifted the white napkin to wipe his mouth, his every movement one of elegance. Jeremy had none of that coarseness of manner so evident in many of our acquaintances. I watched his slim, white fingers caress the stem of his wine cup and flushed as his eyes met mine and I saw the flame of his desire for me.

'That was a meal fit for His Majesty,' Jeremy said. ''Tis a long time since I tasted as good.'

I smiled. 'You were hungry.'

'Yes.' He slid his hand along the table to lay it over mine. 'And glad to be here — with you.'

I felt the burn of his eyes as they went over me, shivering as I remembered the warm taste of his mouth on mine and the way his love-making had brought the slumbering woman within me to life. But even as I yearned to be in his arms, I knew a moment's doubt. 'It has been a long time,' I said, slowly, half accusing. 'I hoped you would write.'

'It was not possible. I was with the King constantly until he fled to the Scots — the traitorous dogs! — and we were ever on the move. Sometimes we went for days without food or even a roof above our heads. We had to move fast because our enemies were always at our heels. Mostly I was too tired to do more than dream of you; but you were ever in my thoughts, Anne. I promise it was so.'

'Then I must believe you,' I said, smiling into his eyes as the candle's glow touched on the gold of his hair; longer than I remembered and curling in love-locks on the lace of his collar. He was very handsome, my cavalier, and his caressing looks were persuasive. 'But tell me your news. We hear little enough at Withington . . .'

Jeremy stroked my wrist with his forefinger, his mouth tightening. 'The King was a fool to trust in the Scots.

He was assured of a treaty when he went to them, sure that they meant to help him regain his throne, but they sold him to Parliament, to his enemies!' His fingers pressed into my flesh, hurting me. I moved slightly and he let me go.

'Doctor Babbage told me the money was owed the Scots for their expenses in the war. Was it not so?'

'It was the excuse they gave,' Jeremy said, bitterness in his eyes as he drank deeply from his wine cup and refilled it from the Rhenish stoneware jug.

His eyes glittered angrily and I saw that his thoughts were far from me. 'What will you do now that the war is over?' I asked, hoping to break this bitter mood.

'The war is not over. The fighting has ceased for the moment, but it will not be finished until His Majesty is restored to his own.'

I stared at him, puzzled by the new hardness in him. He was a man who had tasted defeat and found it gall in his mouth. At this moment I could see little of the charming boy who had won my heart two years since. This was a new Jeremy. When he stared at me so coldly he seemed a stranger: someone I had never known.

'I have heard that Cromwell is trying to reach a settlement with His Majesty. Is that not the truth?'

'Cromwell!' Jeremy's voice was heavy with scorn. 'His Majesty were a fool an he put his trust in that viper.'

'But is he not a man of high ideals? I know he fought against the King — but I have heard he is an honest man.'

'Then confound all such honest men!' Jeremy exclaimed, pounding his fist on the table and causing the wine to spill over. I watched the dark stain as it spread into the starched linen cloth. 'Cromwell is a traitor and will be dealt with as such when the time comes. The army and Parliament fight amongst themselves like a pack of scavenging wolves. His Majesty walks a narrow path between the two, listening first to one then the other — trusting neither.'

'Then what will happen? Do you believe that it must come to bloodshed again?' I felt chilled and sick in my stomach. 'Oh, Jeremy — will it never end?'

Jeremy got up and walked to the fireplace, looking moodily into the embers of the fire. In the silence I became aware of the rising wind outside and the beat of rain against the windows. Even as he stood there there was a tremendous crack of thunder and then the room was lit by a sudden white light as the lightning tore across the sky. I jumped up and went to draw the blinds, shutting out the storm. I felt afraid, though whether 'twas of the storm or what was to come I knew not. Then Jeremy turned to look at me and I saw the uncertainty in his eyes.

'His Majesty believes he can win this dangerous game he plays, Anne; but for myself I doubt it. He is wrapped about by foolish restrictions laid on him by blind, bigoted fools who try to bend him to their will. He will not bend — no, not if they threaten his life. He was born to kingship and duty and he will not flinch from what he believes is right, though he may speak his enemies fair whilst he tests their mettle. If he would but listen to his friends; slip away now to France before 'tis too late. Then we might raise a new army and force Parliament to acknowledge him as King.'

For a moment the room seemed to darken around me and I felt a terrible crushing sensation in my breast. My throat was tight and I could hardly breathe. I was cold and there was a buzzing sound in my ears. I seemed to see a man's pale face. He looked tired and defeated — and I knew he was the King, though I had never seen His Majesty. I felt his agony of mind and I was frightened for him and for my country. For a moment I swayed as the vision in my mind blocked out the familiar comfort of my own parlour, and I clutched at the table edge for support. Then the buzzing in my ears grew less and I could breathe again. I drew my tongue across dry lips, trying to speak normally as I sat down once more.

'Would it not be better for His Majesty to reach an honourable settlement now, even if it meant making some concessions to Parliament?'

Jeremy whirled round on me, his eyes blazing. 'Cry craven and give those miserable bigots best! What kind of a country would England be then? What chance for Catholics to lead a decent life? No, we have to beat them.' He smacked his fist against the wall. 'We have to!'

Suddenly much that had puzzled me became clear. I supposed I should have guessed the truth before — but perhaps I hadn't wanted to. 'You are a Catholic,' I said.

Jeremy stared at me, the fire burning fiercely in his eyes. Then I saw it die away and his mouth twisted in a wry smile. 'Yes — had you not guessed it? I always meant to tell you — but I was afraid of what might happen. I thought you might turn away from me.'

'You need not have been afraid: it makes no difference.'

'Oh, but it does,' he said. 'Because of it they have sequestered my estate — taken everything I own but my sword and the clothes on my back. I have nothing to offer you, Anne . . . '

I stood up and moved towards him. 'I want nothing but your love.'

Jeremy laughed, his mouth twisting wryly. 'So you would live on love alone!' I had reached him now and he touched my hair gently. 'How beautiful you are, Anne, and you have such courage. I almost believe you would take me as I am.'

'You must know I do not care for wealth. My grandfather would welcome you here as a son. There is all we could ever need right here at Withington.'

'No, Anne, I cannot stay here. I have work to do for His Majesty. Even now I am carrying letters from the Queen and others. When the King goes to France I shall go with him.'

I stared at him, the blood draining from my face. 'Then this is good-bye.'

'No.' He caught my hands and held them tightly, a look almost of desperation in his eyes. 'I have tried to forget you for your own sake — but always you haunted me. In my dreams I saw your face and looked into your wonderful eyes — those eyes which called to me wherever I laid my head. Come with me to France, Anne. I will find work as a mercenary until His Majesty returns to England.'

'Oh, Jeremy, I have loved you so much!' Tears caught in my throat as he drew me into his arms, tipping my face so that I looked up at him.

'Why — you're trembling, my love,' he said, frowning. 'I've upset you with all this talk of war.'

'No.' I shook my head, unable to tell him what was in my mind. He wiped the tears from my cheeks, misunderstanding the reasons for them.

'Don't cry, my lovely one,' he whispered close against my hair. 'This parting will not be for long. As soon as my mission is complete I will come back for you. Then we shall be together — at least until the King hath need of me.'

I laid my head against his shoulder, bereft of words. He didn't understand and I couldn't tell him, not tonight while he held me in his arms. He was spinning dreams which had no substance. I could not go to France with him. I could never leave Sir John while he lived. If I had to choose between the two men I loved, then the choice was already made. But I would not tell Jeremy of my decision tonight. Time enough for that in the cold light of morning.

Jeremy's lips moved against my hair and I felt him tremble as he said, 'May I come to you tonight, Anne?'

I lifted my head then to gaze up at him and what I saw in his eyes made my pulses race. For a moment rebellion surged in me: I was young and in love, why should I not take this chance for happiness? I could ride away with my lover this very moment and no one would gainsay me. But in the next instant I knew such thoughts were vain: my own conscience would not let me go. If I deserted my grandfather now whilst he was ill it would haunt me all my days, destroying my love for Jeremy. I must be patient and wait for the war's end and my lover's return in England.

Yet I would not speak of this to Jeremy now. We should have this night of happiness if no more. 'I shall go up now,' I said, smiling at him. 'Come to me soon, my love.'

★ ★ ★

I lay wakeful as Jeremy slept beside me, watching the first rays of a rosy dawn creep through the window. I turned my head on the pillow, gazing on the face of my lover, wanting to trace the faint line of stubble on his chin, to tangle my fingers in his soft hair and press my lips to his, to know again the dizzy joy I had found in his arms last night. He looked so young lying there, his mouth curved in a smile of content, no sign now of the bitterness I had seen in him when we supped together. I bent over him, studying every line of his face, trying to imprint each detail in my mind so that it would never leave me.

Somehow I must have disturbed him, for he opened his eyes and smiled at me, his arms reaching out to pull me close against his chest. I snuggled into the smooth hardness of his body, inhaling the warm scent of him, sighing as I felt his hands move over my back. 'What are you thinking?' he asked, kissing my neck. 'You looked so serious.'

'Nothing.' I lied, my voice muffled in his shoulder. 'Only wondering when you must go.'

His hand caressed the nape of my

neck. 'This morning — but I shall return within the month. 'Twill take me a few days to make the necessary arrangements for the letters I carry to be smuggled into His Majesty; then I must wait for his reply. When all is ready I shall come for you.'

'No.' I pulled away from him and sat up, my face hidden from his view by a veil of dark hair, unwilling to look at him. 'I cannot come to France with you, Jeremy.'

For a moment he lay where he was as though stunned; then he gripped my bare arm, jerking me so that I fell across his chest and was imprisoned there, forced to look into the fury of his eyes. 'What do you mean?' he asked coldly. 'Last night you swore you loved me. Why have you changed your mind?'

I tried to move away but he held me fast, tangling his fingers in my hair to make me look at him. 'I haven't changed my mind. I do love you. You must believe me. If I were free I would follow you this very minute wherever you chose to lead; but I am not free. Sir John is ill: he needs me. I cannot leave him.'

Jeremy's face hardened. 'He may be recovered by the time I'm ready to leave. Besides, he has his servants to care for him. Surely he would understand if I talked to him.'

'No.' I tried to pull away from him again but his fingers were biting cruelly into my flesh. 'You're hurting me! Please let me go.'

'Not until you tell me you will come with me.'

'I cannot. I want to with all my heart, but I cannot.' My eyes begged him for understanding but I could see he was too angry to even try to see my reasons for refusing.

'Why?' His eyes blazed into mine. 'Isn't your love strong enough to face poverty with me in France?'

'Don't — ah please don't!' I begged, flinching as the ice of his scorn seared me. 'Stay here at Withington with me.

Don't make me choose between you. Or if you cannot stay, say that you will come back once the war is finally over. If Sir John no longer lives I will go with you then.'

His fingers dug deeper into my arm and I saw the bitter anger in his eyes. 'It seems you've made your choice, mistress,' he sneered and suddenly flung me away from him, swinging his body round to sit upon the edge of the bed, the sheet still wrapped around his waist. I touched his shoulder, tears starting to my eyes. He couldn't be going to leave me like this.

'Please, Jeremy, try to understand that he needs me.'

He turned to face me then, his face hard and cold. 'You think I have no need of you? Have you any idea of the risks I took to come here?' He snatched the packet of sealed letters he had concealed beneath his pillow for safety and thrust them beneath my nose, his eyes glittering. 'There's enough here to hang me if I'm caught.'

'Oh, please don't!' I cried, tears running down my cheeks as the pain twisted inside me. 'I cannot bear it. I love you. I love you so much.'

'You shouldn't cry,' Jeremy said. 'I hate to see a woman beg. When I was a child my step-father made my mother cry because it pleased him to see her humbled. When I begged her to stop he shut me in the cellars for a whole day. It was so cold and dark down there.'

There was an odd note in his voice and I remembered the times I had heard him cry out in his fever, strange mumblings which had made no sense to me until now. I had never heard him speak of his family before and I stared at him, bewildered by his strangeness. His lips were white, his nostrils flaring as he breathed heavily. I saw that he was shaking, but it was the expression in his eyes which frightened me.

'Why are you staring at me like that?' I whispered, shrinking away from him.

Jeremy did not speak. Turning

320

swiftly, he thrust me back on the bed, holding me as I struggled fiercely. I gazed into his cold eyes and saw the lust there, his mouth twisting with a cruel smile. 'No . . . ' I whispered, my voice hoarse with a new fear. 'Please, Jeremy, don't do this — don't make me hate you!'

He lowered his head, grinding his mouth punishingly on mine so that I tasted blood. How different were the tender kisses of last night from this wanton hurting, this humiliation meant to wound me. I struggled then, fighting him with all my strength, but he hit me hard, making my lip bleed. I twisted and turned beneath him as he thrust into me, trying to escape the cruel battering of his flesh against mine, but to no avail. He took me without mercy and without love, hurting me and seeming to relish the pain he caused me.

After he had done he rose and began to pull on his breeches, behaving as coolly as if nothing had happened. I watched him with dull eyes, hardly realising what he had done to me in my pain. I had given him my love so freely. Surely I had not deserved this from him!

'Why?' I asked at last, my tongue moving over bruised lips. 'Why?'

He looked at me then, and I saw something akin to hatred in his eyes. 'Don't use tears to bind me, Anne,' he said, buttoning his shirt as if everything was as it had been — but would never be again. 'I love you, God knows, but I won't be your slave.'

I shivered. I did not understand this new Jeremy: he was not the man who had won me with his teasing smile. There was a hardness in him that chilled me: he was a stranger I did not know.

He walked to the window, fastening his boot hose and tying the band at his wrists. ''Tis a fine day for travelling. Have you a horse in your stables I can take?'

'Yes — though none as fine as Plato.

What happened to him?' I could not believe we were talking like this.

'He was shot from under me at Rowton Heath; but I managed to catch a trooper's mount: he had no further use for it.' He looked at me as he fastened his baldrick and slipped his pistols into his belt. They were a fine pair of snaphaunces but with the modified English lock called a dog lock, their barrels finely chased and the butts worked with silver. They had been Sir John's parting gift to Jeremy when he rode off to join the King two years ago. 'I shall come back when my mission is complete,' he said. 'You have one month to choose who is more important to you: a sick old man — or me.'

I felt sick as I gazed into his cold eyes. What had possessed me to give my heart to this selfish man? I had been blind. A lovesick, foolish child. I had snatched at the dream of love and now it had turned to ashes in my heart.

'I have already decided,' I said quietly, pride bringing a defiant sparkle to my eyes and a flush to my cheeks. 'I shall not leave Sir John — nor shall I ever come to you.'

'So be it.' Jeremy picked up his hat with its broad brim and curling feather, making me an extravegant, mocking bow. 'Then farewell, mistress. My thanks for the night's lodging. 'Twas as sweet a bed as I have ever lain in.'

With that he walked to the door, opened it and went out.

8

FOR some time after Jeremy left I sat staring numbly at the door, unable to move. In a few short minutes my life had been rent apart, leaving me bewildered and empty. For two whole years I had hugged my secret dreams to myself, planning a golden future with the man I loved . . . had loved, I corrected myself. But even as I made the mental correction, I realised it was not the truth. I still loved the dream I had kept hidden in my heart, for the man I had built my dreams around did not exist. I had never really known Jeremy. How could I when he'd told me so little of himself and nothing of his family? I had let his charming smile blind me to his true nature — though the signs were always there if I had cared to look. I had never wanted to look beyond the smile. If I had been deceived then I was as much at fault as he.

His brutality this morning had left me feeling cold and empty, but I knew that when the first numbness had worn off I should mourn the loss of my dream — if not the man. Perhaps if he had come back then to take me in his arms and beg me to forgive him I would have done so. I could not deny he had cause for his hurt and anger. Yet if he had truly loved me, might he not have understood why I could not go with him? But he did not return and as the minutes passed the coldness inside me became a wall of ice about my heart.

Rising, I poured water from last night's pitcher into a bowl and began to wash. It was cold and made me shiver, but I washed every part of my body, scrubbing mercilessly at my skin as if I could wash away the memory of his touch. Would it could so easily be done!

It was Bessie's baking day, and when

I reached the kitchen she was up to her elbows in flour, busily kneading the dough for the quartern loaves Greta would carry to the bakehouse behind the scullery. A mouthwatering array of pies and pastries bore witness to her industry, and I knew there was no hope of hiding Jeremy's abrupt departure from her. She had obviously been up since first light.

'Ask Polly if the butter's come yet,' she said to Greta, not pausing in her work. 'I'll be needing some for the honey cake later. Oh, and you can take those scraps for the hens whilst you're about it.'

Greta left the hare she had been gutting, picking up the pail of kitchen scraps and going out without a word I noticed her eyes looked red and guessed that Bessie had been scolding her.

'Has Greta been crying?' I asked, when the girl had gone.

'Aye, there's trouble at home. Her sister Tilly has been working over at

Mathews Farm for a twelvemonth, helping to support her widowed mother and the little ones — there's five of them under the age of nine — and now she's been dismissed. Greta's the only girl in work, and her brother has a family of his own to raise.'

'Why have the Mathews dismissed Tilly?' I asked, removing a boiling pan from the heat as it spilled over on to the fire.

'Seems she's got herself in trouble and Croxley found out about it. He made her stand in a white sheet in church last Sunday so that everyone could see her shame. Well, Mrs Mathews decided she'd not have a wanton in her house and turned the girl out that very day. 'Tis my belief she suspects her husband of being the father of Tilly's child, though Tilly won't say who's to blame.'

'That's not fair!' I cried, forgetting my own troubles in a burst of anger. 'Why should Tilly take all the blame whilst the father goes unpunished?'

Bessie shrugged. ''Tis the way of things, Anne. 'Tis always the woman who pays for the man's pleasure.' She looked at me and frowned. 'He's gone then?'

'Yes. I don't want to talk about it, Bessie.'

She placed the bowl of dough beside the fire to let it rise in the warmth. 'Then I'll say no more. I told Greta I'd ask you if we could find a place for Tilly here.'

'Of course we can — there's more than enough for you and Greta to do even with Polly's help. She can help about the house until the baby's born, and afterwards she can help Polly with the milking. You've been saying we need another cow or two. Well, I'll ask Grandfather about it.'

'Aye, then we could make our own cheeses again; 'twud save me traipsing down to the farm so often for milk and butter, too. There's rarely enough for our needs these days.' She frowned. 'That's a nasty bruise on your lip,

Anne! How did you come by it.'

'I slipped and fell against the bedpost.' I turned away to pick up my basket from where I had abandoned it last night. 'I've a deal of work waiting for me in the stillroom, Bessie. Will you tell Greta Tilly is welcome to start work as soon as she likes?'

'I'll tell her,' Bessie said drily, and I knew she hadn't believed my lie. 'Perhaps his going was for the best, lass.'

I walked away without replying. I had never been able to lie to Bessie and it was too soon to think of telling her what had happened between Jeremy and myself. As yet I was able to go about my daily life with an air of calm: I had not so far begun to feel the pain. I was conscious only of the great void the destruction of my dream had left. I shed no tears as I worked steadily through the morning, washing and preparing the plants I had picked yesterday. It was skilful work and needed all my concentration, and

I deliberately pushed all other thoughts from my mind. Later, when I went up to see Sir John, I was able to smile and read to him as usual, but I made no mention of Jeremy's visit and he asked no questions.

★ ★ ★

Outside the wind howled and moaned about the tree tops, sending little gusts of smoke down the chimney and into the parlour. I heard a door open somewhere in the house and the sound of voices, then the parlour door swung wide and Doctor Babbage entered. His cheeks were redder than usual from the cold, and he had a thick woollen muffler wound round his neck. I knew that he must have urgent news to venture out on such a day. I hurried to offer him my chair and draw him nearer to the fire.

He glanced towards Sir John who had been dozing in his chair by the hearth. 'I came straightaway to give you the news,' he said, removing his cloak and holding his hands towards the flames. 'Faith, but 'tis bitter out this day. I swear 'twill snow before morning!'

'Will you take a mug of mulled sack, sir?'

Doctor Babbage smiled at me. ''Tis kind of you, Mistress Anne. I will if Sir John will join me.'

My grandfather looked up and nodded. He was wide awake now, his mind as keen as ever though his body was frailed of late. I bent to tuck the blanket more securely around his legs and he patted my hand and smiled.

'I'll fetch it now,' I said, but Doctor Babbage laid his hand on my arm.

'Tarry a moment and hear my news, Mistress Anne.'

'What news?' Sir John growled. 'What have those devils in London been up to now?'

''Tis the King . . . he's escaped.'

Sir John's eyes lit with new life and

he gave a cry of fierce triumph. 'God be praised! 'tis what we've prayed for! Come, man, tell us more. How did he escape and when was it?'

'Escaped!' I stared at him. 'Has His Majesty fled to France?'

Babbage turned to me, puffing out his checks importantly. ''Tis not known for sure — but they are searching for him everywhere. The ports are being watched, but in my opinion it's already too late. He'll not have wasted time: he'll be safe in Jersey or on board a French ship by now, you mark my words. This has not been a spur of the moment affair. Yes, he'll be halfway across the Channel whilst the Levellers hunt for him in the forests and rant of plots and bribes. Some say Cromwell was involved in the escape.'

'Cromwell? Never say it. Where did that tale spring from?' Sir John had leaned forward in his chair, his eyes glowing with an eagerness I hadn't seen in many a day.

I took the chance to slip away to the

kitchen, my mind wandering through the tangled maze of my thoughts. So the King was gone to France and Jeremy with him. I might have been on that ship even now if I had wanted. At this moment I felt a pang of regret for what might have been. There were days when I remembered the sweetness of my lover's smile, and there were lonely nights when I forgot his selfishness.

Bessie was alone when I entered the kitchen, busily peeling the vegetables for our evening meal. She looked up and seeing my expression she frowned. 'What ails you, Anne? You're trembling.'

'Am I?' I sat down on the stool she pulled out for me and took a deep breath. 'It was just a little sickness. I shall be better in a moment.'

Bessie pursed her lips. ''Twill be a mite longer than a moment if I'm any judge — and you'll be worse afore you're better.'

I looked up, startled by something in her tone. 'What do you mean?'

'There's no need to lie to me, child. You'll need help when your time comes.'

I felt the colour rise in my cheeks and I was tempted to deny it, but I should have realised I could not keep my secret from Bessie's knowing eyes. 'How long have you known?'

Bessie sniffed. 'I wasn't sure until a moment ago, though I've suspected as much for a while now. But 'tis not the babe making you look like that. What's happened to upset you?'

'Doctor Babbage says the King has escaped; they think he may have gone to France.' I clasped my hands together to stop them shaking. 'Captain Allenby will join him there — if he is not already with him.'

'He doesn't know about the child?' Bessie gave me a hard look.

'No.'

'Is there no way you can reach him?'

'No.' I raised my eyes to hers. 'Nor would I if I could.'

'Then what's to do? What will you do when your time comes?'

'I don't know.' I twisted the strings of my girdle. 'I must hide it for as long as I can. Perhaps Aunt Sophia will help me. You know she has always wanted me to go to her. Perhaps we can go away together for a time. I should have to go somewhere quiet where no one knows us. How does one conceal these things? I once heard Sarah talking about her friend's daughter who was in similar difficulties. She came back later and no one knew what had happened.'

'Aye, your aunt would help you, though there's the babe to consider. You'd have to find a good woman to take the child and rear it as her own.'

I stared at her. This was the first time I had thought about the child as a living being. Until now I had tried to pretend that it did not exist, to push it from my mind with the memories I preferred to forget. I had stopped trembling and I stood up. 'There's time enough to decide what must be done — I must take Doctor Babbage his mulled sack or he'll think I've forgotten him.'

'Bide you there,' Bessie commanded, her voice gruff to hide the affection she felt for me. 'I'll see to it — and a little cowslip wine would do you no harm.'

I laughed. 'Dearest Bessie, don't fuss or you will betray me; and don't look so worried! I'll manage somehow.'

'Aye, I dare say you will.' Bessie hung a blackened pot over the fire, adding a pinch or two of the sweet herb hanging from the beam above her head. 'But you should try to contact Captain Allenby. He has the right to know about his child. If he's a grain of decency in him he'll marry you.'

'Do you think I would beg him to wed me?' I raised my head to look at her with glittering eyes, my pride touched. 'No, I shall never tell him — never! He has forfeited any right to that knowledge.'

Bessie sighed and shook her head at me. 'You were ever a stubborn lass. What did he do to hurt you so?'

'Enough!'

Bessie took up a large iron ladle and poured the hot, sweet wine into two mugs, setting them on the table. 'I knew the day would turn out ill,' she muttered. ''Twas only to be expected. The portents are bad.'

I looked at her curiously. 'What do you mean?'

'Strange things have happened hereabouts lately,' she replied, crossing herself with a hasty glance over her shoulder. 'The hound of hell has been heard baying in the woods, and Joe Prichett saw a carriage pulled by headless horses passing the church at midnight. 'Tis a sure sign of trouble ahead.'

Bessie seemed really worried and I felt a cold shiver run down my spine, just as I had when Jeremy told me of the King's plans for a new war. Normally I laughed when Bessie repeated this kind of gossip from the village, but this time I could only pretend to scoff.

'That's superstition — you don't really believe it.' I smiled slightly. 'Joe Prichett was probably in his cups.'

'Aye, mebbe he was,' Bessie said sniffing. 'But I've heard the hell hound myself — 'tis a fearful sound no living creature could make. Besides, I feel something bad is coming . . . ' She broke off as Greta's sister came into the kitchen, carrying a pile of mending.

Tilly was very near her time now. She moved slowly, her body awkward and heavy. When she saw me her eyes lit with a warm smile and she came to sit beside me at the table. Since I had taken her in Tilly regarded me as her saviour, and in a way perhaps I was. With five small children of her own to feed Tilly's mother would probably have turned her from their little cottage to fend for herself. Girls who bore illegitimate children could expect to be dragged before the magistrates, and sometimes received a whipping for their

339

sins; but even those who took them in could often be fined for doing so. Croxley had come to warn me of the risk I ran by harbouring a wanton, but I smiled and spake him fair and he left in a better temper than when he came. So far I had not been called before the magistrates to pay my fine, but if the worst happened I would pay it and keep Tilly beneath my roof. However, I believed myself safe for the moment. The county magistrate was Sir Mathew Attwood, and I was almost sure that I might expect an offer of marriage from his nephew at any time. Once I had refused it I might no longer be safe from prosecution, but I did my best to keep the young man from speaking, wishing to offend neither him nor his uncle.

Now I stood up and laughed a little shakily. 'Your hell hound is probably a hungry dog, Bessie; and as for your premonition, Babbage says there'll be snow before nightfall. Surely that's bad enough!' I picked up my tray with the steaming hot wine. 'I had better take this before the good doctor dies of thirst!'

★ ★ ★

It was growing dusk as I left the farm, having stayed longer than I'd intended. Sally Lucas had kept me talking, and the younger children crawled on to my lap begging for stories, their dark eyes straying all the while to the basket of gifts I had brought with me. In a few days it would be Christmas, and experience had taught them that the basket would be full of good things; sweetmeats, nuts, small toys and cakes. This time there was a tiny doll for the youngest girl and the head of a hobby-horse for the eldest boy, to which Nat would fasten the long stick and tail he had hidden in the storehouse.

I was feeling relaxed and happy as I waved to Sally from the brow of the hill and saw her vanish inside to the warmth of the kitchen. Since the birth of Sally's last child we had become good friends, and I enjoyed my visits to the farm. I loved having the little ones clamber into my lap to be hugged and kissed, or simply snuggle into the crook of my arm while I told them stories of dragons and princesses in far-off lands.

I was thinking now of my own child as I walked slowly home. As yet my secret was safe, for I had let out the seams in my gowns and no one seemed to have noticed I was gaining weight. Sir John was often too sunk in apathy to even realise I was there unless I spoke, and neither Sally nor Mercy would dream of the reason behind the change in my figure. Tilly might have guessed it from her own experience, but she was approaching her time and suffering badly in these last few days. I knew that I could not hope to hide my condition for much longer, before the spring it would be only too obvious. I had already written to Aunt Sophia asking her if she could spare us a brief visit, but she said Sir Thomas was ill and she could not leave Barnwell Hall for the present. I prayed he would be well again before the spring!

I could ask Mercy to stay at Withington whilst I was absent. I should need to be away for several months, but then I could come home again and no one the wiser. Except that I was determined to keep my child. It had taken me many hours of agonising to reach my decision, for the deception would not be an easy one. As the granddaughter of Sir John Taverne I might perhaps escape the whipping meted out to other less fortunate girls who had born a bastard child, but I should not escape the censure of my neighbours. I could look for no more courtesy calls from eager widowers, nor from Sir Mathew's nephew. I might find this easy enough to bear, but my friends would also have to bear the disgrace if they wished to go on visiting me. No, I was coward enough to fear complete social disgrace, and honest enough to admit it. Somehow I must conceal my shame even if I had to pretend the babe was an orphan given into my care by its dying mother. This was why I so badly needed my aunt's help. Whilst my word might be doubted hers would not.

Such a story was bound to cause gossip, but if we were careful there would be no proof. At least I should be able to keep my child, and this was most important to me. Although the memory of my last parting with Jeremy was something I would rather forget, I longed to hold my child close to my breast. My child: not his. Not ever his.

'Good-even', Mistress Taverne.'

Lost in my thoughts I had hardly noticed the shadowy figure moving towards me through the twilight. I stared into the wrinkled face of the old woman who was deliberately blocking my path.

'Good-evening, madam. I don't believe I know you?'

She was dressed all in black, her gown frayed at the hem and badly patched. On her head was a black cap from beneath which straggled wisps of greasy, grey hair, and around her shoulders she clutched a filthy shawl. Her face was thin and drawn, unnaturally white as if she spent her days shut away from the sunlight.

She drew back her lips from toothless gums in the travesty of a smile. 'But I know you, mistress. I know where you go and why. I know everything about you!'

I frowned in perplexity. 'I don't understand,' I said. 'Who are you?'

The woman made an odd chuckling sound which made my blood run cold. 'She doesn't know me but I know her. I've watched her many's the time.'

Suddenly I remembered all those unnerving occasions when I'd felt that I was watched — and the flash of a black gown as someone disappeared inside the church.

'Have you been following me? Not

just today but many times? Was it you in the churchyard that day — and in the woods?'

The woman nodded her head, her dark eyes glittering with excitement. 'I've watched you wherever you go. I never let you see me but I'm always there.'

'Why?' I stared at her, bewildered. 'Why should you want to spy on me? What do you want of me?'

She tipped her head on one side, considering me with bright hawklike eyes. 'Shall I tell her? No, not yet: 'tis my secret. She has secrets, but not from me.' She gave a cackle of laughter.

There was something chilling about the old woman, a look in her eyes which seemed to menace. 'Who are you? Why — why do you hate me?' For she did hate me, I could feel it.

Even as I spoke a change came over her; her eyes glittered with a fierce light and her hand shot out, gripping my arm with her long talons. She pushed her face close to mine so that I recoiled from the foul smell of her breath, and she peered at me with those birdlike eyes. Then she brought her other hand up to touch my head, chortling with a malicious glee as she tore a strand of hair from my scalp. I jerked my head away, giving a cry of pain.

'What have you done?'

'I've broken your power; that's what I've done!' She showed me the hairs she'd plucked from my head, her face glowing with a kind of evil triumph. 'Your magic was too strong for me, but I have you now!'

I stared at her in bewilderment. 'What are you saying? I don't understand you.'

'You can't hide from me,' she hissed angrily. 'I know you for what you are. My spells were useless against you, but now I have what I need. I've cursed you time and time again but you refused to die. This time you shan't escape me.'

I gasped, drawing back as I gazed into

her malevolent eyes. 'You — you're a witch!'

She chuckled again, nodding her head with glee. 'A black witch. Once I was a white witch like you; but that was before I sold my soul to the Devil. I made a pact with the Evil One in return for power — the power to destroy you!' Her voice rose to a hysterical scream.

I felt her hatred choking me. It was all around me, filling my lungs, my mind and smothering me. I found it difficult to breathe. There was an aura of such evil around the old woman that it terrified me. I drew a deep breath, trying to still my shaking hands as I looked at her. 'Why do you say I'm a white witch?'

'I've seen where you go and what you do, and I know your strength. I've felt it in here.' She tapped her breast with those twisted claws.

I stared at her, feeling the sickness sweep over me as the smell of pine and gorse stirred long buried memories from the dark reaches of my mind. 'Who are you?' I whispered, but already I knew the answer. 'Why do you hate me so?'

'I'm called Mother Black Cap — but 'tis not my given name. I was born Meg Green and I had a brother — Will.' Her eyes glowed like burning coals in the pallor of her face as she pointed a skinny finger at me accusingly. 'You killed him!'

The blood drained from my face and I swayed dizzily. 'No,' I whispered. 'It's not true. I did not kill him!'

'I can see things others cannot.' She pushed her face close to mine again. 'You were the cause of his death. I have the gift of 'Sight' and I know Will died the night he disappeared. You were there. I saw your face in my vision as clearly as I see you now. You were there when he died! Deny it if you can!'

I saw the glittering of her eyes and I passed a hand across my face, trying to block out the knowledge of such hatred. 'I cannot deny that I saw him die; but he brought death upon himself. He attacked me and he tried to kill . . . someone else.' I hesitated, catching my breath as I recalled that terrible night. 'Will was insane!'

'Liar!' she shrieked, lunging at me with her talons crooked. I twisted away bare seconds before her claws went for my eyes. She gave a scream of rage and went for me again, but I pushed her hard and she stumbled, losing her balance and falling. The next moment I was past her and running. I heard her cry out as she rose to her feet, shaking her fist at me. 'I've cursed you, Mistress Taverne. I've cursed you and all your family. There's no escape — no escape for any of you.'

I did not look back as I heard her frenzied cries. I was running for my life, frightened by the malevolence in her eyes and the viciousness of her attack. How she must hate me to have nursed her grievence so long, watching me from afar, planning her revenge. I ran in sheer, blind panic long after I had left her far behind. I was panting for breath and gasping as I let myself into the house. As I staggered into the kitchen, I was trembling from head to foot, half afraid she was close behind me waiting to tear out my eyes with her yellowed claws.

Bessie looked at me in alarm as I sagged against the wall. 'What ails you, Mistress Anne? Are you ill?'

I shook my head, sinking on to the stool she pulled out for me. 'No, I've just had a fright, that's all. I'll be better in a moment.'

Bessie touched my hand, frowning. 'Why, lass, you're shaking. What is it?'

'She's white as death,' Tilly said.

They both looked at me in concern as I struggled for breath. I was beginning to feel better now surrounded by the familiar comfort of home and my friends. 'It was so foolish,' I said, forcing myself to smile and sip the cordial Tilly brought me. 'I was frightened at nothing . . . '

'Drink up, lass, and get your breath.' Bessie ordered, and I was grateful for her solid presence.

'An old woman who called herself Mother Black Cap threatened me . . . ' I knew even as I spoke that I could not reveal the whole truth. 'She attacked me as I walked home.'

Bessie's plump face paled and she crossed herself swiftly. 'Lord have mercy on us! 'Tis as I feared: she means you harm.'

Tilly gasped. 'Why that old crone! A witch she be, mistress, and mazed in 'er mind I reckon.'

I looked up at them. 'She said she is a witch — and that she's cursed me and all my family.'

'The wicked old biddy!' Tilly cried. 'She should be hanged for her evil doings so she should.'

'She's the blackest witch this side of hell,' Bessie moaned rocking the table as she plumped down on a stool. 'I did my best to keep her from you.

You didn't let her touch you?'

She touched my arm,' I said, trembling at the memory. 'And I think she pulled some hairs from my head.'

Bessie frowned. 'Then there's no time to be lost, Anne. You must make water and bring it to me in a clean vessel.'

I stared at her, bewildered. 'What do you mean?'

'Bessie's right, mistress,' Tilly said. 'If you've been cursed your urine must be boiled together with clippings from fingers and toes at midnight — and the Lord's prayer must be chanted backwards at the same time.'

Bessie was nodding. I looked from one to the other. 'You don't really believe she has the power to curse me, do you?'

'She be a wicked, evil one, mistress. I heard tell she ill-wished Goody Pearson's cows and they dried up their milk over night. You do like Bessie says and break the spell.'

'Please, Anne, laugh at me if you will, but please do as I ask.' Bessie took the corner of her white apron and wiped her eyes.

I had never seen Bessie cry before and the effect of her tears was startling. Until now I had been certain witches were merely wretched old women forced to live as outcasts by superstitious villagers, but now I was not so sure. My experience tonight must have frightened me more than I realised. Mayhap it was all foolishness, but it could not harm to take what precautions we could. I nodded. 'If — if it will please you I'll do as you ask. And there's rosemary and marigold heads in the jars in the stillroom. I'll sew them into a linen bag to wear inside my . . . ' I faltered as a groan broke from Tilly.

Bessie and I both turned to look at her. She was leaning against the table and gasping. Her face was twisted with pain as she clutched at her belly, moaning.

'Oh Lord, it hurts,' she screamed, her lips drawing back in a grimace of pain.

Bessie was on her feet at once. 'There's no need to panic, child, just take a deep breath and it will pass in a moment.'

Tilly looked at her, her eyes wide and scared. 'Is it time, Bessie?'

'Aye, I reckon so by the looks of you, but it will be a while yet. I'll call Greta from the dairy and she can help you to bed. There — it's going now as I said.'

Tilly nodded, smiling slightly. 'Yes, 'tis easing now. I'm sorry to make so much fuss. Oh God! Bessie, Bessie, help me!' Tears were starting to her eyes as I got to my feet.

'I'll fetch Greta. You take Tilly upstairs, Bessie, and stay with her. Greta and Polly can see to the supper. I'll come up in a while, Tilly, and we'll do what we can to make it easier for you.'

'Thank you . . . ' Tilly was panting

hard as Bessie put an arm around her and drew her from the room.

I took up a lanthorn and went out into the yard. Greta would be washing the pans in the dairy but they could wait until the morning. She would be needed now to set pans of water on the fire and fetch and carry. It was going to be a long night by the looks of things.

It was to be one of the longest and most terrible nights of my life. Tilly's pains were strong from the first, but as the hours wore on they became worse and worse. At the start she tried to be brave and we teased her along, tying a sheet to the bedrail so that she could grip on tightly when the pains came. But soon they intensified so much that she was screaming in her agony, her face a ghastly mask shiny with sweat. I bathed her forehead and held her in my arms, holding a sweet cordial to her dry lips. She swallowed a little gasping out her thanks and seizing my hand as the convulsing pain tore through her once more.

'Help me,' she screamed. 'Ah, God have mercy on me. I did not mean to be wicked; 'twas out of kindness I did it. I felt sorry for him . . . ' She screamed again. 'Forgive me . . . forgive me . . . '

Tears were streaming down her cheeks. I clasped her hand in mine, feeling the sting of my own tears. 'Don't cry, Tilly dear,' I whispered. 'I know you're not a wicked girl.'

She clung on to my hand in desperation. 'Don't let me die, Mistress Anne. I swear I didn't mean to sin that day; 'twas just the way he begged and pleaded made me do it. I've heard tell you can save those you care for. Please help me. Please!'

'I've no special powers, Tilly, but I'll do all I can for you,' I promised. 'I'm going to fetch something for you to drink. It's supposed to bring the babe quicker. Will you take it?'

Tilly nodded eagerly, clinging to my hand so that I had to pry her fingers apart before I could leave her.

I hurried down to my stillroom, my fingers clumsy as I hurried with the preparation of my mixture. I did not know if it would hasten the birth of Tilly's child for I had only recently discovered it in a faded journal which had belonged to some long ago Taverne lady; but it contained a tiny portion of poppy juice and I knew it would ease her terrible agony. The labour might go on for some hours as yet but she would not feel it quite as keenly.

I had to run the gauntlet of Polly and Greta's anxious questions, but at last I could return to the exhausted girl's bedchamber. As I entered the room Bessie turned to look at me with horror in her eyes. ''Tis too late, Anne,' she said. 'She's past wanting that now poor lass!'

I stared at the bed. Tilly was lying motionless, the sheets stained with a great pool of blood, and between her thighs the head of the child she had died strugging to bring into the world. 'But she can't be dead!' I cried. 'The child's half born — a little longer and it would have all been over . . . ' I turned to Bessie. 'The child — can't we pull it away from her? It might still live.'

Bessie shook her head. 'Look closer, Anne. Look at its head. 'Tis a monster — it killed her . . . '

I gazed fearfully at the bed, seeing now the huge head which had split Tilly apart and caused the haemorrhage. I felt my knees go weak and the room span round as I vomited into my apron. 'Oh God . . . ' I whispered. Poor, foolish little Tilly — and she only did it because she was sorry for him.'

I wiped the vomit from my mouth as Bessie pulled the covers over the horrific sight. 'Let it die with her,' Bessie said. 'Tell no one else, Anne.'

I nodded, depositing my soiled apron with the other bloody cloths in a pail. Bessie had obviously fought valiantly to try and stem the flow of blood, but her efforts had been in vain. I felt the silent tears cascading down my cheeks. 'Mayhap we could have saved her together,' I whispered. 'She begged me not to let her die . . . '

''Twas not your fault, Anne. I have known for some time that it would not be an easy birth. We did what we could for her. Perhaps it was a judgement on her.'

'Don't say that!' I cried, my voice rising shrilly. 'Tilly wasn't a wicked girl. She just had a kind heart. If it was a punishment for her sin — then I shall die, too, when my time comes.'

Bessie stared at me. 'Forgive me, lass,' she said wearily. 'I had forgotten for the moment. Of course it wasn't a judgement. I'm tired.' Then she bowed her head and buried her face in the apron stained with Tilly's blood, her shoulders shaking. 'I did what I could for her.'

Bessie was crying. Loud, noisy sobs which shook her plump body. My dependable, unshakeable Bessie was sobbing as if her heart would break. I put my arms around her, whispering what words of comfort I could. 'It wasn't your fault, Bessie, you did what you could for her . . . '

Bessie shuddered, then pushed me away from her, wiping her wet cheeks. 'Go down and tell the others now,' she said. 'I'll make all right here — and Greta can come up when I've finished.'

'I'll stay and help you,' I said, repressing the revulsion I felt as I glanced towards the bed.

'Nay, lass, I'm all right now,' Bessie replied, giving me a slight smile. ''Tis not fit for you — besides, 'tis the last I can do for the poor girl. You go down to the others. I'll not be long . . . '

* * *

My head was aching again. It was so bad it almost blinded me, blurring my vision and making me vomit with the pain. I had had it for three days now — since the morning after Tilly died. That afternoon I had walked into the village to make the arrangements for her burial. Croxley had refused to give

361

her a Christian burial at first, but after much persuasion I had finally got him to relent. Tilly would be laid to rest this afternoon. I must be there to witness it: I had to fight off this headache somehow.

For most of the morning I'd been lying on my bed, but now I felt I must make the effort to get up. Soon it would be time to leave for the funeral. Soaking a kerchief with lavender water I held it to my nose, inhaling the sharp sweetness of its fragrance. I glanced at my reflection in the mirror, frowning as I held it closer to look at myself. My face was flushed and I had dark rings beneath my eyes. I hadn't slept well since Tilly died. I could not help wondering if she had died because of me — because of the curse laid upon me and mine by Mother Black Cap. I knew it was foolish, but her death had followed so close after that frightening meeting with the witch — and Tilly had been like a part of my family. Although she'd spent such a short time with us her good nature had won all our hearts. It was so unfair that she should go to an early grave!

'Superstitious nonsense!' I muttered, scolding myself. And yet there was this terrible headache which would not go away.

I laid the mirror down, sighing. Life could be very cruel sometimes. Tilly was dead because she had felt sorry for the father of her child. I had given my love to a man who had existed only in my dreams. Would I be punished for my sins, too? I had never before feared childbirth, though I knew it was always hard, but now I wondered if I should die.

'What a fool you are, Anne Taverne! What would Colonel Lawrence think of you now? Starting at shadows.'

I laughed as I remembered the night Christian Lawrence had tried to chase away my fears for Sir John with his talk of witches. He would think me a fool to fear the curse of a mad old woman.

What had made me think of Christian

Lawrence? I had not seen him since that night and did not expect to. Shrugging, I picked up my kerchief and pressed it to my forehead. I wished the pain would go away if only for a little while.

I left my room and went down to the parlour. As I neared the open door I heard the sound of Doctor Babbage's voice and almost turned away. I did not feel like making polite conversation just now. Then I heard my grandfather's reply and something in his voice made me pause.

'But how can I tell Anne? She's upset by the death of that girl — and it's nearly Christmas.' His voice quavered and shook. 'It will break her heart — and mine — to tell her.'

'You cannot hope to hide it from her much longer, my friend,' Babbage replied with a heavy sigh. 'She will have to know the truth soon.'

I went into the parlour, noticing Sir John's guilty start as he saw me. I crossed over to his chair, kissing his cheek and smiling at him. 'Good-morning, Grandfather. Good-morning, Doctor. What shall I have to know soon?'

They exchanged expressive glances, and I saw a flicker of pain pass across my grandfather's face. Then he slumped back in his chair, all the resistance ebbing out of him as he said, 'Tell her, Babbage; I cannot.'

I felt a pang of fear as I looked from one to the other. Sir John was obviously incapable of dealing with the situation whatever it was, and the doctor's face reflected his own distress. I knelt beside Sir John's chair, taking his frail hand in mine and feeling it tremble. 'What is it, sir?' I asked, looking into his face. 'Surely you can tell me. Is it Prudence?'

'No,' Sir John groaned, forcing the words out painfully. 'I've failed you, my child — your inheritance is lost!'

His hands were shaking violently. I held them tightly, willing him to go on. 'I don't understand you.' He shook his head, emotion robbing him of speech. I looked up at Doctor Babbage. 'What does this mean?'

Babbage cleared his throat nervously, obviously dismayed at Sir John's distress. 'Your grandfather has to pay a large fine levied on him by Parliament because Saul fought on His Majesty's side . . . ' He paused, reluctant to go on.

My head was throbbing and his face misted before my eyes, but I had to know the whole truth. 'I've heard that many of the King's followers are being served thus. We are fortunate in not being Catholic else we might have lost all . . . ' My voice trailed away as I saw Babbage's expression. I stood up, lifting my head proudly. 'Please tell me everything, sir.'

Babbage puffed out his cheeks. 'Your grandfather mortgaged part of the land to contribute to His Majesty's cause. What with the interest on the loan and this fine added to the loss of harvest during the war . . . '

Sir John raised his head, looking

into my eyes with something of his old pride. 'We must sell Withington, Anne.'

'Sell the house!' I was stunned. Never had I expected anything as terrible as this. 'Sell our home!'

'You won't be penniless, Mistress Taverne,' Babbage put in hastily. 'I've managed to get a good — nay, a generous offer for the house, the farm and what remains of the home pasture. 'Tis twice as much as you might have expected. Sir John will be able to pay his debts and the fine and still retain a reasonable competence. Especially if you make your home with me as I've suggested to this stubborn fellow here.' Babbage's voice choked with emotion and he had to turn away to blow his nose.

'No.' Sir John growled with a flash of his former pride. ''Tis good of you, Babbage, but we shan't be paupers. We'll find a cottage somewhere.'

I rested my hand briefly on his shoulder. Walking to the fireplace I stood with my back to them both, struggling to control my emotions. Until this moment I had known nothing of Sir John's financial difficulties and the shock was considerable. It would be a great wrench to leave my home, but the thought of my grandfather being forced to spend his last days in poverty was intolerable. My own feelings at this moment were as nothing beside his. I felt his pain and humiliation as a physical ache in my breast. Turning, I smiled at him despite the hammering in my head. 'You should not have been afraid to tell me, Grandfather. I have often thought this house too large for us, but I would not mention it while you were content to live here. We shall do well enough in a cottage like Mercy's.' I frowned as the thought struck me. 'What will happen to Mercy and the Lucas family? They will not lose their homes?'

Sir John could only shake his head at me, overcome.

'No, no, my dear,' Babbage reassured

me. 'Sir John has secured Widow Harris's cottage to her for life, and the new owner of Withington intends no changes in the estate. Indeed, he has behaved like a true gentleman throughout. You are not to feel you must leave Withington immediately, Anne. His agent has stressed there is no hurry, no hurry at all.'

I swallowed hard, trying not to think of a stranger at Withington. 'When does he want us to leave?'

'No date has been set. You are free to make what arrangements you will.' He looked at me anxiously. 'I wish you will consider my offer, Mistress Anne. I should be glad to have both you and Sir John as my guests — if only for a time.'

My head was spinning. The pain had intensified and I was beginning to feel really ill, my whole body burning up. I tried to smile at Babbage but was forced to sit down rather suddenly on the settee as my legs gave way beneath me.

Sir John roused from his apathy to look at me in alarm. 'What is wrong, Anne?' He glared at Babbage as if blaming him. 'The shock has been too much for her.'

I moved my head in denial, moaning at the pain it caused me. 'No. I've been feeling ill for some days.'

Babbage bent over me in concern. 'With your permission, my dear.' He placed his hand on my hot brow. ''Tis as I thought; you are burning with a fever. There is much of it in the village. I was called to the Lucas children only yesterday. Have you visited there recently?'

'Three days ago.'

'Then you took it from them.' Babbage sounded relieved. ''Tis unpleasant but not fatal if care is taken. You must go to bed at once.'

'But Tilly . . . '

'I will attend in your stead. I insist you rest, Mistress Anne.'

I felt too ill to resist. 'Please tell Tilly's mother why I could not come.'

I stood up, swaying unsteadily as I looked at Sir John. 'Please don't worry, Grandfather. We will talk when I'm better.'

Sir John nodded, his face grim. Unable to rise from his chair without Hoddle's assistance, he was frustrated by his inability to help me. I knew how great his humiliation must be at losing our home, but I could find no words to reassure him. At this moment nothing seemed to matter but the throbbing in my head. All I wanted was to lie down and close my eyes.

9

I WAS ill for several days, during which time the good doctor called regularly to see me even though Bessie would not let him examine me for fear he should discover my secret. But he was happy just to gaze at me benevolently and assure himself I was no worse, for the fever was virulent and he had no wish to take it himself.

Bessie nursed me herself, using my own cures for cooling a fever and hanging bunches of garlic above my bed to protect me from witches. She was still convinced my illness was caused by Mother Black Cap's curse.

However, after a few days I began to feel much better, though I was disinclined to do much more than sit by the fire and read my favourite poetry at first.

Christmas had come and gone whilst

I was ill, but in any case we had received no invitation from my aunt this year, which puzzled me as it was her habit to send a letter and some small gift. Prudence did send presents and a brief message, making no mention of her newly-born daughter — of whose birth we learnt from Philip very formally. I was afraid my sister was still unhappy.

Babbage rode over to tell us the King was a prisoner on the Isle of Wight, whence he had foolishly fled instead of escaping to France. Nat Lucas had injured himself in a game of football on Boxing Day, a mighty rough affair in which all the village participated. Croxley had denounced it as the Devil's own game, promising his congregation eternal damnation if they did not mend their ways; and the parish constable carried off the worst offenders for drunkeness. Meanwhile the weather was bitter cold, the thick snow cutting off Withington from the village since neither horse nor oxen could get up the hill.

Confined to the house, I spent my time wandering aimlessly about the rooms, touching things. I wondered how many of these possessions, which were precious only because of their familiarity, I could take with me to our new home.

Bessie watched me anxiously, guessing only part of what was in my heart; and poor Greta went about with red eyes and an even redder nose as she struggled with a heavy cold.

Finding her weeping in the scullery, I tried to comfort her. 'Tilly wouldn't want you to cry, child.'

Greta smothered a sob, wiping her nose on her apron. ''Twasn't our Tilly's fault. 'Twas Farmer Mathews done it to her. Old Goody Canham seen them. Why should he get off without so much as a word from parson and Tilly's dead? I ain't never goin' to let a man touch me. Never!'

Looking at her pale, thin face, I doubted if she would ever know the temptations her plumper sister had experienced. Few men would plead with Greta for her favours. I wondered what would become of my little scullery maid when we were forced to leave.

Three weeks after Christmas the snow cleared and Babbage rode over to see us, having made inquiries about a suitable cottage for us.

'I cannot see you will be able to afford a house of any size. If only Sir John had spoken to me earlier.'

'He has been so ill — and Sarah's death changed him.'

'I know.' He patted my hand. 'I don't mean to criticise him. 'Tis a sorry thing to see him so low.'

'We are fortunate to have you our friend, sir, for I do not know how we should manage else. A cottage will do so long as there's room for Hoddle. Grandfather needs him.'

'I'm not sure you can afford him, my dear.'

'We must, even if it means doing without something else.'

'Then I shall help you; Sir John need never know.'

I saw him to the door, realising it was time I told my servants I might soon have to part with them. However, Hoddle became very emotional, declaring he would rather die than leave his master and would work only for his bed and the food he ate.

I was deeply touched by his devotion, promising we would pay what we could.

Bessie swore nothing but the grave would induce her to leave me. 'I've a little money put by; 'tis yours if you need it.'

I turned away to hide my tears, but their loyalty had helped me to face what must come. It would hurt me to leave my beloved home, but somehow I would hide my sorrow from my grandfather.

As the snow melted and the first spring flowers appeared my spirits lifted. I began the task of sorting linen and Sir John's books. Babbage had told me the new owner would buy any furniture I didn't want. And as the days passed I grew curious about the new occupants.

'Is it a big family?' I asked Babbage. 'It would be nice if there were children here again.'

I thought wistfully of the cot in the nursery where I had hoped to lay my own child. Pressing my hands to my belly, I felt the swell of new life and was comforted.

My waist had thickened considerably and soon my condition must become apparent — I was afraid Babbage had already begun to suspect, though he would be loth to think so ill of me. I had written to my aunt again for I was worried by her unusual silence. Although we didn't often see each other, the posthorn had sounded regularly at my gate.

Babbage frowned as I pressed him for an answer. 'I don't know the gentleman's circumstances, Anne. I have dealt only with his agent. But you will meet him yourself next week, for his agent wrote to say he intends coming down to settle the last details himself.'

'I see.' My heart sank. 'No doubt he wishes us to leave. I think we must settle on the cottage you told me of.'

''Tis not what I should like for you.'

'No — but we have little choice.'

'You could stay with me — just until you find something more suitable.'

'And when would that be?' I sighed, knowing Sir John would never agree. 'You have already done too much for us.'

'Nonsense.' The doctor's chin wagged. 'I like not the thought of you and my old friend in that place — this move can only . . .'

I saw his face contort with emotion. I knew that he believed the move would kill Sir John, as I did.

'Oh, why can't he die in his own bed?' I cried bitterly. 'Why must he suffer this humiliation?'

Life was so unfair and the bitterness was in my mouth as I turned away to glance out of the window. The flowers were just beginning to push through the reddish earth, but I should not be here to see them bloom this year. It was all because of the war; because the King had lost and our new masters were determined to make his friends suffer. How I hated them and all their ilk!

'You could speak to him when he comes, Anne.'

I whirled around and fear and anger made me cry out: 'Why should he let us stay, this stranger who comes to claim his property? Withington is his now.'

* * *

It was a crisp January morning. Little icicles clung to the branches like sugar frosting on a cake, and the brief taste of spring had gone. My breath froze on the windows, tracing intricate patterns on the glass, and I shivered despite my shawl and the extra petticoats I had donned.

Resuming my seat on the settle tucked into a corner of the open fireplace, I took up my needlework and tried to concentrate on the tiny gown I was sewing, thinking it was fortunate my sister had recently been brought to bed of a daughter. Not that I feared the tongues of my servants.

It was impossible to concentrate. Putting down my work, I went back to the window. The frost was melting a little and I watched a droplet of water slide slowly down a stem of trailing ivy and fall with a plop to my windowsill. The slight thaw would not help travelling conditions, for the roads would be soggy and treacherous. So perhaps he would not come today, after all. Mayhap he would wait until the spring and by then it might not matter so very much.

Sir John was failing day by day. Often he would speak of Sarah as if she were still alive. Perhaps the present was too painful for him to contemplate. If only we could stay just a little longer.

I heard voices outside the parlour door and my heart stopped beating for one terrible moment. I recognised the doctor's laugh and I knew he had brought Withington's new master to see me. I remained at the window, afraid to turn round as the parlour door opened and I felt a rush of cold air at my back.

'Mistress Taverne,' Babbage said, 'this is the gentleman you have been waiting to meet.'

I turned slowly, gasping as I saw who was with him. The shock drained the colour from my cheeks, leaving me with no words of greeting. For if there was one man in the world of whom I could not beg the smallest favour it was he.

'Mistress Taverne.' The grey eyes were thoughtful upon my face. 'Forgive me — I returned from abroad only last week. I had no idea my agent had bought Withington.'

'I see.' I could not meet his steady gaze. 'I hope you are not disappointed in . . .'

'No, no,' he assured me quickly. 'Withington is a fine house. I was merely surprised Sir John agreed to the sale.'

'If you will excuse me, I shall look in on Sir John.'

Babbage retreated, leaving us to stare at each other in silence.

'Will you not come to the fire, sir?' I asked, remembering I was still the hostess for the moment. 'I will send for wine unless you wish to tour the house at once?'

Christian shook his head. 'I have seen most of it.' His mouth was grim as he reminded me of the day we first met. He took off his hat and doeskin gloves, laying them on the table. 'Why are you selling? Because of the fine?'

His blunt question surprised me. 'How did you know of that?'

'I made it my business to do so.'

I turned away so that he should not

see my face. 'No, it isn't because of the fine. Withington is too big for us.'

He was silent for a moment, then I heard a soft sound and turned to find him standing close behind me. I looked up into his searching gaze. 'Don't lie to me, Anne. You have to sell, don't you?'

'Yes,' I said haughtily, 'Sir John mortgaged the lands to help His Majesty and now . . . '

'My God! this damned war has much to answer for. It must be killing him to leave here.'

'It is — I think he will not survive the move.' I pressed my hand to my mouth, holding back my cry of pain.

'I'm sorry. You have suffered unnecessarily. Naturally you will both continue to live here for as long as you wish.'

The concern in his voice overset me. I moved away to the window as the tears flowed silently down my cheeks. 'You are generous, sir,' I said in a voice so low he must have strained to hear it, 'but we could not live here as your pensioners.'

He was silent and I wondered if he had heard me, then: 'Could you bring yourself to live here as my wife, Anne?'

The shock of his words held me rigid. I closed my eyes, trying vainly to stop the tears squeezing through my lashes, but they trickled down into my mouth as I spoke. 'As your wife?'

Christian smiled wryly. 'Are you really so surprised? You must know I have a great regard for you.'

My hands were shaking and I felt sick. I had not guessed it but I should have. Oh, if only I had not been so stupid and so wicked! He was offering me my dearest wish but I knew I could not take it.

'Please do not, sir. You are kind but . . . ' My voice trailed away to a whisper.

'But we were enemies. Is that what you would say?' He looked at me sadly. 'Last time we met I thought you had forgiven me. Could you not accept friendship from me, Anne?'

With every word he spoke he shamed me more. I shook my head, hardly knowing how to face him. 'Ah no — it is too much, sir. I am shamed by your goodness.'

He frowned. 'Why should you be shamed? I meant no offence. Such a marriage would pleasure me much.'

There was no way out for me. I could not lie to him nor send him hence believing me ungrateful. I brought my eyes up to his, though it cost me much. 'You honour me greatly, sir. Alas, I am not worthy of your regard. I carry in my womb the seed of the man who was your enemy — the man you once vowed to kill.'

I saw his eyes travel over me with new awareness and heard his harshly-drawn breath. He moved away from me to stare into the flames. I neither moved nor spoke as I waited for him to look at me with the coldness I knew I must now see in his eyes. I had behaved no better than a wanton and his regard for me would turn to disgust: and it would be no more than I deserved. Then he came back to gaze down into my face and I saw not hatred but pain in his eyes.

'Why does this man not wed you?'

'I have not told him, nor shall I.'

'Why?' He studied my face with great intentness.

'I do not wish to wed him. I loved but a dream and the dream vanished when I awoke.'

'Then marry me.'

'You're asking me to be your wife — still?'

I stared at him in disbelief. I had expected scorn, contempt — but never this.

'Yes, I am asking you to be my wife.' I saw his hand clench briefly on his sword hilt as if some fierce emotion raged within him.

'Why?'

'Because . . . ' He hesitated as if torn between the truth and lies. 'Because I need a wife — and I have chosen you. A good marriage can sometimes come from mutual respect. My own parents were betrothed in the cradle. They were content. I believe we might be so.'

If he had sworn he loved me I would have sent him away, for I wanted no more of that false emotion which only served to blind its victims and bind them with chains. Prudence had wed for love and I knew how sorely she regretted her marriage. I had loved Jeremy, but he had never truly loved me. No, I wanted no more of love.

The witch had cursed me and perhaps I deserved no less, for Will had surely died because of me. And yet I might escape her net even now. I looked up into Christian's eyes and I knew that I should take the chance he offered.

'Then — then I should be honoured.'

He smiled, a slow deep smile which lit a flame in his eyes. 'We shall be wed as soon as it can be done.' He frowned. 'Sir John will not forbid it?'

I shook my head. 'He is no longer the man who ordered you from his house — he lives in the past.'

'I am sorry to hear it,' Christian said, and yet there was a gleam of satisfaction in his eyes. 'We must pray he lives to see his great-grandchild.'

'If not he will at least die in his bed. I shall not forget how much we owe you.'

His face hardened and I saw a muscle beat against his throat. 'I do not want your gratitude, Anne.'

I gazed up at him, and a tiny shiver of fear went through me. 'What do you want of me, Christian?'

For a moment his eyes burned into me and I thought he meant to crush me in his arms. A tiny cry escaped my lips as I moved away to prevent him. What had I done? I had given my promise to this man and I believed he had tricked me. For a moment I wanted to run away — far away before it was too late. But where had I to run?

I was trapped. Trapped by my

promise and my need of him. He knew it and he would keep me to my word.

'What do I want?' he asked softly, his brows lifting as he smiled mockingly. 'Why — what should I want but a good and dutiful wife?'

I shivered, afraid of him now as I had been the night he killed Will. And yet he dominated me now as he had then. I had not the strength to send him away, and I knew that I would be his wife because he willed it so.

I should be his wife, his property — just as Withington was. The property of a man who should rightly be my enemy. The future loomed dark and frightening before me, but I was caught up in a great wind and I could only go where the wind carried me.

'I will try,' I said, 'to be a good wife.'

Other titles in the Linford Romance Library

SAVAGE PARADISE
Sheila Belshaw

For four years, Diana Hamilton had dreamed of returning to Luangwa Valley in Zambia. Now she was back — and, after a close encounter with a rhino — was receiving a lecture from a tall, khaki-clad man on the dangers of going into the bush alone!

PAST BETRAYALS
Giulia Gray

As soon as Jon realized that Julia had fallen in love with him, he broke off their relationship and returned to work in the Middle East. When Jon's best friend, Danny, proposed a marriage of friendship, Julia accepted. Then Jon returned and Julia discovered her love for him remained unchanged.

PRETTY MAIDS ALL IN A ROW
Rose Meadows

The six beautiful daughters of George III of England dreamt of handsome princes coming to claim them, but the King always found some excuse to reject proposals of marriage. This is the story of what befell the Princesses as they began to seek lovers at their father's court, leaving behind rumours of secret marriages and illegitimate children.

THE GOLDEN GIRL
Paula Lindsay

Sarah had everything — wealth, social background, great beauty and magnetic charm. Her heart was ruled by love and compassion for the less fortunate in life. Yet, when one man's happiness was at stake, she failed him — and herself.

A DREAM OF HER OWN
Barbara Best
A stranger gently kisses Sarah Danbury at her Betrothal Ball. Little does she realise that she is to meet this mysterious man again in very different circumstances.

HOSTAGE OF LOVE
Nara Lake
From the moment pretty Emma Tregear, the only child of a Van Diemen's Land magnate, met Philip Despard, she was desperately in love. Unfortunately, handsome Philip was a convict on parole.

THE ROAD TO BENDOUR
Joyce Eaglestone
Mary Mackenzie had lived a sheltered life on the family farm in Scotland. When she took a job in the city she was soon in a romantic maze from which only she could find the way out.

NEW BEGINNINGS
Ann Jennings

On the plane to his new job in a hospital in Turkey, Felix asked Harriet to put their engagement on hold, as Philippe Krir, the Director of Bodrum hospital, refused to hire 'attached' people. But, without an engagement ring, what possible excuse did Harriet have for holding Philippe at bay?

THE CAPTAIN'S LADY
Rachelle Edwards

1820: When Lianne Vernon becomes governess at Elswick Manor, she finds her young pupil is given to strange imaginings and that her employer, Captain Gideon Lang, is the most enigmatic man she has ever encountered. Soon Lianne begins to fear for her pupil's safety.

THE VAUGHAN PRIDE
Margaret Miles

As the new owner of Southwood Manor, Laura Vaughan discovers that she's even more poverty stricken than before. She also finds that her neighbour, the handsome Marius Kerr, is a little too close for comfort.

HONEY-POT
Mira Stables

Lovely, well-born, well-dowered, Russet Ingram drew all men to her. Yet here she was, a prisoner of the one man immune to her graces — accused of frivolously tampering with his young ward's romance!

DREAM OF LOVE
Helen McCabe

When there is a break-in at the art gallery she runs, Jade can't believe that Corin Bossinney is a trickster, or that she'd fallen for the oldest trick in the book . . .